THE KNIGHT
NEXT DOOR

THE KNIGHT NEXT DOOR

•

CHARLENE BOWEN

AVALON BOOKS
THOMAS BOUREGY AND COMPANY, INC.
401 LAFAYETTE STREET
NEW YORK, NEW YORK 10003

© Copyright 1997 by Charlene Bowen
Library of Congress Catalog Card Number: 97-93726
ISBN 0-8034-9244-8

PRINTED IN THE UNITED STATES OF AMERICA
ON ACID-FREE PAPER
BY HADDON CRAFTSMEN, BLOOMSBURG, PENNSYLVANIA

To Vicky,
with love

Chapter One

To a casual observer, there wasn't anything to set Cole Wyatt apart from the genial assortment of customers in the Four Star Diner. He responded in kind whenever an off-handed remark was directed his way, and even offered an occasional comment of his own.

On closer inspection, though, there was something about him—a barely perceptible reserve—that kept him from being a part of the easy camaraderie that was going on around him.

"You ready for a refill, hon?" Billie, the plump, too-blond waitress, smiled at him across the counter, her coffeepot poised. "How about some apple pie? I could put it in the microwave and warm it up." Her manner gave the impression that her primary aim in life was to see to Cole's well-being and comfort.

Billie's term of endearment and solicitous tone weren't lost on the other customers. Several eyebrows raised in amusement, and one grizzled cowboy grinned knowingly and nudged the person on the next stool.

"No thanks, I have to get going." Cole drained his cup and stood up. If he was aware of the little stir of amused interest generated by Billie's none-too-subtle attentions, he gave no indication. As he dug a handful of crumpled bills out of his pocket, he nodded to the three ranchers who were lingering over coffee in a booth down past the end of the counter.

"Wyatt, you ever decide on that new bull you were thinking of buying?" one of the men, Wes Detweiler, asked.

"Not yet," Cole replied. "I'm still looking."

"I heard Sam Harding, over in Lake County, has some good Hereford stock," Henry Collins put in. "You oughta go see him before you—" He broke off in mid sentence, his jaw dropping in surprise.

Several heads—including Cole's—turned to follow Henry's line of vision. Cole didn't notice anything unusual out the front window. The only thing he saw was a compact car he didn't recognize pulling into the parking lot across the street. Nothing especially unusual about that. Even in this remote corner of southeastern Oregon, an occasional stranger passed through town, usually someone who had taken a wrong turn off the main highway.

As the door of the car opened and the driver got out, Cole glanced at her curiously. He saw nothing about her to merit the kind of interest she seemed to be generating among the customers in the diner. She appeared to be hardly more than a teenager. Her pale blond hair was pulled back from her face in a ponytail, and the loose-fitting T-shirt she wore with her faded denim jeans emphasized her slight build. She couldn't have been much over five feet tall.

Just before she turned and headed toward the small office building with a neat sign next to the door that read: WARREN EAGLETON, ATTORNEY AT LAW, she paused and took a long, slow look around her. Cole couldn't make out her features very well from this distance, but he had an impression of large, deep-set eyes in a delicate oval face.

Although Cole made a practice of keeping to himself as much as possible, in a town the size of McClintock, everyone had at least a nodding acquaintance with everyone else. She didn't look at all familiar, so she must not be a local girl. He wondered what she was doing here. She was much, much too young to be driving these back country roads by herself, he thought, with a stab of disapproval. She looked too . . . too . . . The word that came to mind was *vulnerable*.

Not that it was any concern of his, he reminded himself. As he waited for his change, he became aware of the murmur of voices, low and speculative, around him.

"It *is* her." This was said in a tone that bordered on disbelief.

"I wouldn't have thought she'd have the nerve to show her face around here."

"She does have a right to." The words came out hesitantly, as if the speaker was reluctant to go against the tide of disapproval. "This is her home."

"Hah! She couldn't even be bothered coming back to see her parents buried."

"You know her uncle Frank explained all that—about why his niece Nadine had to go ahead and make the funeral arrangements."

"All I've got to say is that whole story about Frank and Nadine not knowing where to reach her sounds mighty fishy to me." This was accompanied by a scornful snort.

"I wonder if she's back for good."

"I doubt it. She'll probably just stay long enough to get the ranch sold."

In keeping with his usual habit of ignoring gossip, Cole paid as little attention as possible to the conversation swirling around him. Still, he couldn't keep certain phrases from penetrating his consciousness. The person under discussion would be Jamie Cantrell, he realized. Her parents, Trace and Carolyn, had been his nearest neighbors until their deaths in a plane crash a few weeks ago had stunned and saddened the small, close-knit ranching community. They'd been on their way to a cattle buyers convention in Boise, and their small Cessna 172 had run into a sudden, unexpected storm.

At the mention of the probable sale of the Cantrell spread, several heads swiveled toward Cole. Although he liked to keep his affairs to himself, it was fairly common knowledge that he had expressed interest in buying the Circle C, which adjoined his own ranch.

Sensing that he was about to be pulled into a discussion he had no desire to participate in, he collected his change, dropped a few coins on the counter, and slipped out the door before anyone had a chance to start asking him questions. He didn't have any information to pass along, anyway.

" 'Bye now," Billie called after him. "Come in again— soon." She managed to interject a wealth of meaning into that last word, to the obvious amusement of the other patrons.

He paused outside the diner, taking stock of the situation. He still had several more stops to make, including a trip to the library to stock up on the books and videos that helped him while away his solitary evenings. He'd have to be quick if he hoped to get his errands done and be on his way without being drawn into the gossip and speculation surrounding the girl.

Woman, he amended. Obviously he'd been mistaken in his original impression that she was barely out of her teens. Despite his attempts to stay aloof from the talk going on around him, he hadn't been able to completely shut it out. Bits and pieces of things he'd heard came back to him. By the time that—that trouble had taken place, she'd already been teaching at the local elementary school for a couple of years, and the whole affair had happened before he came here. He'd been in McClintock five years, so that would make her in her late twenties, at least. It must have been her small stature that had made him assume she was younger. Or maybe it was just that from his vantage point of almost forty, everyone seemed terribly young.

He couldn't recall just what kind of scandal she'd—supposedly—been involved in. He had a vague memory that it had something to do with Frank and Nadine Palmer's daughter, Sheila, and Sheila's husband, Randy. Funny, from that brief glimpse he'd had of her, she didn't appear to be the home wrecker type.

His lips quirked into a wry smile. What had he expected, anyway—that she'd have a scarlet letter emblazoned on her forehead?

Of course, considering the town's propensity for embellishing a story, there was always the possibility that she hadn't committed any of the wrongs attributed to her. He reminded himself of how easily the whole affair—whatever it was—could have been blown out of proportion. He couldn't suppress a brief stab of sympathy for this woman he'd never even met. Who knew better than he what it was like to be falsely accused?

He pushed the subject from his mind. His only interest in Jamie Cantrell had to do with whether she would accept the offer he planned to make on the property she was inheriting from her parents. With his own ranch doing well now, he could afford to think about expanding. And the logical place to start would be by buying the Cantrell spread, now that it looked as if it might be available. He'd already talked to Hank Adams down at the bank about getting an extension on his loan.

"Jamie, I can't tell you how delighted I am to see you," Warren Eagleton said. "You've been away too long."

When Jamie had hesitantly tapped on the door of Warren's office, she hadn't been sure of just what kind of reception to expect, even though during her growing-up years he'd been more than just her parents' lawyer. He and his wife had also been close friends of the family. Still, others whom she'd considered friends had been all too ready to believe the ugly gossip that had circulated about her.

Warren's welcome, though, had been warm enough to dispel any doubts. "Jamie, it *is* you!" he'd exclaimed, engulfing her in a warm hug. Then he held her at arm's length, scrutinizing her.

"Hmm. You're way too thin, but just as pretty as ever. You're getting to look more and more like your mother."

At the mention of her mother, a shadow crossed Jamie's face. Seeing this, Warren said, "Jamie, I want you to know how sorry I am about your parents."

She swallowed the sudden lump that was making it difficult for her to speak. "I—I wish I could have gotten back in time for the funeral—"

"I know you'd have been here if I'd been able to reach you. Your folks told me you were no longer in Portland, but they neglected to put your new address in with their important papers. I tried to hold Frank and Nadine off until I could locate you, but they insisted it wasn't decent to wait so long to give your folks a Christian burial. I finally had to let them go ahead and make the arrangements.''

Jamie blinked back the tears that sprung to her eyes. ''What's done is done.''

''So—tell me what you've been up to lately,'' Warren said, tactfully changing the subject.

''Well, as you already know, I'd been teaching fourth grade in Portland. I didn't really like big-city life, though. Then I heard about this small school district just east of Jordan Valley, that was badly in need of a teacher. They were having a hard time finding anyone who wanted to live in such a remote area. I applied for the job, and the next thing I knew, there I was—with a grand total of ten students, from kindergarten through sixth grade. I hated to leave them in the lurch, but fortunately they were able to find someone to take over when I got your phone call.''

''When do you have to be back?'' Warren asked.

''I don't. My substitute has promised to stay until they can find someone permanent.''

Warren considered this bit of information, but made no comment on it. ''I'm sure Marianne will be as delighted as I am to see you,'' he said, reaching for the telephone. ''I'll call and have her get the guest room ready.''

''You don't need to do that.''

''Surely you're not thinking of staying at the hotel? It'd be like living in a fishbowl.''

''I'm not going to stay there. I've already dropped my things off at the ranch.''

Warren's features wrinkled into a frown of concern. ''You won't want to be out there all alone, will you?''

''It's not as if I'm in a strange place. It's my home,'' she reminded him softly.

''But—'' Warren started to protest, then apparently thought better of it. ''Now then,'' he said, ''it's time to get down to business. The Circle C belongs to you now, of course. Several people have expressed interest in buying it, and I've had one firm offer.''

''Oh, but I'm not planning to sell.''

Warren gave her a searching look. ''You know, Jamie, as your friend as well as your lawyer, it's my duty to play devil's advocate,'' he said. ''Do you really think you could run the place by yourself?''

''Why couldn't I? I've already talked to TJ. He's willing to stay on—he says he's been there too long to start looking for work somewhere else.''

There hadn't been much question of whether TJ Weber would stay, of course. He'd signed on as a young cowboy, and had worked his way up to the position of foreman. Now he and his wife, Val, and their three sons were comfortably settled in a roomy house on a section of Circle C land. It wasn't likely he'd want to move his family.

''And I think most of the hands will stay if TJ does,'' Jamie went on. ''Oh, I know a few of them have already found other jobs, but I can always hire some new men.''

Warren shook his head doubtfully. ''Some of the men might stay out of loyalty to your folks, but you might have trouble finding enough hands to get up a full crew.''

''Why? Don't you think they'll want to work for a woman?'' There was a touch of defiance in her tone.

Warren cleared his throat. ''That's not the reason, Jamie, and you know it as well as I do. It's just that—well, folks around here have long memories.''

''I guess that's just a chance I'll have to take,'' Jamie replied. But despite her air of bravado, there was a little prickle of apprehension inside her.

''Since I can't talk you into staying with us, you'll at least come over for dinner this evening, won't you? Marianne will want to see you.''

Jamie hesitated. "I'd really like to, but there's so much I need to get caught up on at the ranch. I still have a few more stops to make while I'm in town. I need to do some grocery shopping—and I want to run by the library and see if they've got a copy of *The Stockman's Handbook*. The bookstore doesn't have any on hand right now, and Dad's copy is so tattered it's falling apart. I'll take a rain check on that dinner, though." With a promise to let him know if there was anything she needed, she was on her way.

She hoped she could slip into the library and back out without encountering anyone. To her relief, the building was almost deserted except for an elderly man who had nodded off in one of the easy chairs in the reading section.

The only other person in sight was Miss Dowling, the birdlike little woman who had presided over the library ever since Jamie's high school days. She glanced up briefly as Jamie, keeping her face averted, hurried past the desk.

Jamie was back in a few minutes, having discovered that certain areas of the library had been rearranged. In spite of her wish to remain as unobtrusive as possible, she reasoned that it would make more sense to simply ask for assistance than to waste valuable time trying to figure out the new layout.

She stopped short and ducked back between two rows of shelves as a tall figure clad in denim jeans and a brown plaid shirt came in the front door. Although she couldn't make out his features from this distance, she was fairly certain he wasn't anyone she knew. Still, she didn't want to take a chance on any unexpected encounters.

He was hardly inside the building when Miss Dowling spoke up. "Oh Mr. Wyatt," she said, "I—I'm so glad you came in. The latest book by that author you're so fond of just came in. I know you didn't ask for a hold on it, but I put it aside for you. And we have a new video I thought you'd like, so I saved it for you. I—I'll just get them.''

When she started to get up, her elbow bumped against a stapler on her desk, knocking it to the floor. As the resulting clatter echoed through the silence, the old man who had been dozing awoke with a start and glanced around in surprise. With trembling fingers, Miss Dowling picked up the stapler and replaced it before retrieving the book and video from a shelf behind her desk.

"Thank you," the tall man replied, shifting his weight from one foot to the other as he accepted the items she handed him. "That was—ah—very thoughtful of you." Jamie thought he seemed a little embarrassed, as if he'd prefer not to be singled out for special attention.

The librarian flushed a bright pink. "It—it was nothing," she replied, her soft voice sounding slightly breathless.

Jamie realized that, by trying to remain unnoticed, she had made herself an unwilling spectator to this little exchange. If she moved at all she would draw attention to herself.

She could do nothing but stand there between Reference and Adult Fiction, and watch as Miss Dowling stammered and blushed like a schoolgirl. It was obvious the woman was absolutely smitten. Studying this Mr. Wyatt, Jamie wondered why he had such an effect on the normally staid little librarian. Although she couldn't see his face from this angle, there seemed to be nothing about his tall, lanky frame or his almost diffident manner to evoke that kind of reaction. Except for his exceptional height, he seemed quite ordinary. There was no accounting for tastes, she thought with a shrug.

"I'll just—ah—look around and see what else I can find," he said to Miss Dowling. With that, he beat a hasty retreat toward the Mystery section. Jamie couldn't help noticing the look of longing on Miss Dowling's face as she watched him walk away.

As the librarian returned to her desk, Jamie let her breath out slowly. The incident she'd just witnessed had served as a reminder that there was no telling who might come wandering in. Oh, she knew she was going to have to face people before long, but she just wasn't ready quite yet Forgetting her intention of asking for assistance, she turned and headed back in the direction she'd come from. She doubted if Miss Dowling would be much help right now, anyway. The poor little woman was so undone she likely wouldn't know the difference between the Dewey decimal system and Morse code.

Heading toward the back of the library, Jamie couldn't quite control the urge to quicken her steps. As she reached the end of the aisle and hurried around the tall shelves, she came smack up against what seemed to be a solid wall, with such force that she was almost thrown off balance.

When she found herself staring at an expanse of brown plaid, she realized it wasn't a wall she had run into, but the Mr. Wyatt who had put Miss Dowling into such a flutter.

She found she had to tilt her head back to see into his face. "Excuse me—" she began, but the words died on her lips. Something deep inside her told her she'd been seriously off the mark in her original assessment of him as "quite ordinary."

All at once it was clear to her why Miss Dowling had displayed such uncharacteristic behavior. Maybe from across a room the man was unremarkable, but up close he exuded an air of masculinity that was quite overwhelming. Jamie sensed that it wasn't something he did on purpose, or even had any control over. She had the feeling he was completely unaware of the effect he had on women.

In an attempt to bring her scattered thoughts into some kind of order, she focused her attention on his face.

It was an interesting face—not handsome in the usual sense of the word, but there was something arresting about it. Maybe it was the firm, uncompromising line of his jaw, or those deep grooves that ran down either side of his mouth. Smile lines? Not likely, she thought. The bushy eyebrows, drawn together in a frown, reinforced her impression that he was a man who didn't smile much. She wondered if the frown was caused by having been run into so abruptly, or if that was his habitual expression.

She felt no surprise when her glance rested briefly on the faint scar just under one eye. Somehow, it seemed to go with the rest of the face. Continuing the quick assessment, she found herself looking into a pair of piercing blue eyes. The thought hovered fleetingly that the owner of those eyes must be the loneliest man on earth.

"What—" A muttered exclamation left Cole's lips before he had time to realize that the object which had apparently tried to bowl him over was not some sort of guided missile, but a very small person.

A person of the female persuasion, his senses told him, as he automatically put his arms out to steady her—but definitely *not* Miss Dowling.

Everything in him reacted instinctively. It had been a long time since he'd held a woman, especially one as soft and feminine as this one. Her slender curves, pressing against the hard planes of his own body, caused his heart to lurch erratically.

It took him only a second or two to realize this was the Jamie Cantrell who had elicited so much attention—most of it derogatory—from the patrons at the Four Star Diner.

There was no doubt about it—despite her diminutive stature, she was not the "child" he'd first thought her.

The top of her head came barely to his shoulder, and her hair smelled clean and fresh. If he had been of a poetic turn of mind he might have likened the scent to ". . . flowers after a spring rain." Since he wasn't, he was simply aware that it was extremely pleasing.

Hardly realizing what he was doing, he held her for a fraction of a second longer than was absolutely necessary, enjoying the sensations generated by having this small bundle of femininity in his arms.

As common sense returned, he resisted a sudden, unexpected urge to pull her even closer. He dropped his arms as if he had touched something hot.

"I—I'm sorry," Jamie apologized, her voice shaky. "I should have been paying more attention to where I was going. I was in a hurry—"

"No harm done," Cole replied, trying to keep his tone from betraying the sudden jumble of emotions whirling around inside him.

No harm done, except that this woman, in one brief, chance encounter, had effectively pierced the wall of indifference he'd carefully erected around himself.

Cole tried to pull his scattered thoughts into some kind of order. *Forget it,* he told himself. She'd bumped into him by accident, and he'd instinctively put his arms around her to keep her from falling. And it had made him remember how good it felt to hold a woman. So what? All that meant was that he was spending too much time by himself.

With a nervous smile and another murmured apology, she backed away and went around him, continuing on her way. The whole encounter was over in seconds. Yet the scent of her hair still lingered, and Cole felt a vague sense of loss as he recalled the way she'd felt in his arms.

Chapter Two

During the long drive out to the ranch, Cole did his best to put the incident in the library out of his mind. He concentrated instead on the conversation he'd had with Warren Eagleton last week. He'd stopped in to ask if the Cantrell ranch was likely to go up for sale soon.

"I wish I could give you something concrete to go on," the silver-haired attorney had said, "but there's not a whole lot I can tell you until I hear from Jamie."

"There isn't any way you can get in touch with her and let her know about my offer?" Cole had asked.

Warren shook his head regretfully. "According to her uncle, Frank Palmer, her last teaching job was in some small town out in a remote area. I'm sure she gave her mailing address to her folks, but I haven't been able to locate it."

"The Palmers would have it, wouldn't they?"

"I'm afraid not," Warren replied. "It seems Trace and Carolyn didn't pass that information on to them."

Cole found it odd that Jamie's relatives wouldn't know how to contact her, especially in McClintock, where keeping abreast of everyone else's doings was a major form of entertainment. And family ties were strong around here.

Lowering his gaze, Warren hesitated, as if he felt that some kind of explanation was in order, and was trying to decide how much to reveal. "The truth is," he said at last, "there—ah—wasn't a whole lot of love lost between Jamie and the Palmers, even if they were her aunt and uncle."

After several moments, he resumed his usual business-like manner, giving Cole the feeling he realized he'd come dangerously close to overstepping his professional bounds. "As soon as I locate Jamie, I'll be sure to pass along your offer," he said briskly. "I have no idea what her plans are, of course, but I think she'd jump at the chance to sell. Under the circumstances, I doubt if she'd want to come back and run the place herself. . . ."

Cole hadn't bothered to ask what those "circumstances" might be. Whatever had taken place to make Warren feel that Jamie Cantrell wouldn't care to move back to McClintock, he'd prefer to not hear the details.

As he drew nearer to his own ranch, the roadway narrowed until it was little more than a dirt track. The countryside was growing more rugged now. The broad expanse of land stretched wide in all directions, broken occasionally by shaggy pinnacles and flattop buttes. He eased the pickup around a curve that snaked between two outcroppings of rock. As he came out into the open on the other side, a panorama of sagebrush-blanketed valleys and ridged canyons lay before him, dotted here and there with groups of grazing cattle.

He felt the now-familiar sense of pride when the neat black and white sign that marked the turnoff came into view. LUCKY HORSESHOE RANCH, it read, and below that, in smaller letters, were the words, Proprietor, Cole Wyatt.

Even after five years, the thrill of ownership hadn't faded. It had taken a lot of hard work, a lot of self-denial and sacrifice to get where he was today. Of course, that small inheritance left to him by an uncle he'd never even known had helped. The unexpected windfall, added to what he'd already saved, had been just enough to enable him to make a down payment on the Lucky Horseshoe.

As he drove into the yard, a short, stocky figure glanced out of the barn, then ambled over to the pickup.

Levi Hull, opinionated, occasionally testy, and gossipy as an old woman, was sort of a permanent fixture around the ranch. He'd worked here most of his life, and when Cole bought the place, he hadn't even considered not keeping the old man on. Although Levi's movements were slow and arthritic these days, and he couldn't perform many of the duties the younger hands could, Cole found his commonsense advice and his knowledge of ranching invaluable. And he was a wizard at keeping the various pieces of ranch machinery in good repair. Besides, Cole was genuinely fond of the old fellow.

"Howdy, boss," Levi greeted him in his gravelly voice, as Cole alighted from the truck. "You remember to get all those parts to fix the irrigation pump?"

"I got everything on your list. We can get started on it any time you're ready."

Levi nodded approvingly as he glanced at the items in the truck bed. "Anything interesting going on in town?" he asked, reaching for one of the packages from the hardware store.

Cole gave him a curious look. "Nothing that I can think of. Why?" He had no intention of mentioning the incident in the library—not that there was even anything to tell. So he'd had a chance encounter with the Cantrell woman, and her closeness had ignited a sudden, unexpected fire in him. He wasn't about to let anyone know the effect she'd had on him.

Levi shrugged one shoulder in a gesture of unconcern. "No reason. Just making conversation."

He obviously had something on his mind, Cole thought. No hurry. He'd come out with it soon enough. Sure enough, when they were in the shed a few minutes later, putting away the parts for the pump, Levi remarked, in an elaborately casual tone, "Jamie Cantrell's back, you know."

"That's what I hear."

"Saw her this morning when I was out checking fences. She was looking over her property, so we stopped and passed the time of day."

Cole continued arranging the pump parts on the shelf, where they'd be in easy reach when he was ready for them. He wasn't sure what the old man was getting at.

"She's staying over at the Cantrell place."

The brief nod with which Cole acknowledged this bit of information belied his surprise. Although he'd expected that she would want to have a last look at her old home before selling it, he'd assumed she'd be "putting up" at the town's one hotel. It wasn't as if she was going to be here very long. Most likely, as soon as she could arrange for a quick sale, she'd be leaving. The knowledge that she would be staying on the neighboring ranch gave him an uneasy feeling. Now that he was aware of the emotions she stirred in him, his every instinct warned him to stay as far away from her as possible.

"You going over to talk to her about selling?" Levi asked, breaking into his thoughts.

After a pause, Cole replied, "No, I wasn't planning to."

"Once that ranch goes on the market, competition'll be

keen,'' Levi pointed out. ''There'll be a lot of folks wanting to buy the place. You got the jump on 'em though, so to speak, by living right next door. If you was to go have a talk with Jamie, neighbor-to-neighbor, instead o' going through Warren Eagleton, you could likely come to an understanding.''

Cole rubbed his chin thoughtfully. ''I don't know, Levi. I've already spoken to Warren, and I think it might be more—more businesslike if I were to let him make the initial offer.''

''You're missing a great opportunity,'' the old man persisted.

''Levi, I don't even know the woman.'' That was true, of course. Even here in cattle country, where informality was the order of the day, an unintended collision by no means constituted anything resembling an introduction.

Besides, something told him she valued her privacy as much as he did his. The way she'd slipped back into town after more than five years, for instance, apparently without letting anyone know of her arrival, indicated that she didn't care to have her personal affairs bandied all over the county.

He could respect that. He was, himself, a private person by nature, and circumstances in his life had made him even more so. When he'd moved here, he'd had some vague idea that he could stay out on his ranch and keep pretty much to himself. After all, ranching was more or less a solitary undertaking.

He supposed most folks would call him antisocial, but he'd learned, early in life, that it didn't pay to get too close to people. It just led to disappointment. As a sort of ''defense mechanism,'' he'd developed a cool, noncommittal attitude that had always been fairly effective in warding off unwanted overtures of friendship.

He'd hardly gotten settled in, though, when a steady stream of local folks began dropping by. It seemed that everyone was curious to see who'd bought the old Lucky Horseshoe spread. Despite his attempts to maintain some distance between himself and his new neighbors, he'd been besieged with invitations to various social functions, or to "come over and have supper with us," or "stop by for a cup of coffee when you're in the neighborhood."

It had taken more tact than he usually exercised to extricate himself from all the invitations without offending anyone. Even if he'd *wanted* to become friendly with his neighbors, he wouldn't have been quite sure how to go about it. He was uncomfortable around most folks he came into contact with, although he had developed a grudging fondess for Levi, and a respectful working relationship with the other hands in his employ. And he'd become friends with his closest neighbors, Trace and Carolyn Cantrell. He'd felt a real sense of loss when they were killed in that plane crash.

Gradually, the people of McClintock had come to accept that he was "something of a loner" and, for the most part, they respected his preference for solitude. He was vaguely aware that the general opinion among the townsfolk was that he was *a nice enough feller* but *likes to keep to himself.*

"Well, what about it, Boss?" Levi's voice broke into his thoughts.

"What about what?" He realized, with some embarrassment, that Levi had asked him something, but he'd lost the thread of the conversation.

"Jamie Cantrell," Levi prompted. "If you don't go over and make her an offer, someone else is going to beat you to the punch."

"That's a chance I'll just have to take. I'd rather let Warren handle any negotiations."

Shaking his head, Levi rolled his eyes upward, as if beseeching the heavens for patience.

It wasn't just the memory of the feelings Cole's chance encounter with Jamie had stirred in him that accounted for his reluctance to have any dealings with her. He made a concentrated effort to have as little to do with the opposite sex as possible.

The truth was, most females scared him half to death. He never knew what to expect from them. For most of his adult life women had been subtly—or sometimes *not* so subtly—paying him more attention than he was comfortable with.

For instance, whenever he went into the Four Star Diner, Billie started batting her eyelashes and swaying her hips in a way that was downright embarrassing. Oh, he knew she kidded around and made flirty remarks with all the male customers—that was just her way—but she seemed to overdo it with him. And he wished she wouldn't always *hover* over him, refilling his coffee cup almost before it was empty, and heaping his plate with extra-large portions.

And then there was Miss Dowling at the library. Every time he went in there, she almost fell all over herself in her eagerness to do whatever she could to please him.

He was genuinely puzzled as to why women behaved that way around him. He knew he couldn't, by any stretch of the imagination, be called handsome. For one thing, he was way too thin—almost to the point of gauntness—with an angularity of form that was accentuated by his height.

His face? Well, he'd never had any illusions about it. Like his body, it seemed to be all planes and angles. His sandy brown hair, which he kept trimmed in a no-nonsense short clip, was likewise nondescript. And with that faint scar down one side of his cheek, that still hadn't completely faded after all these years, he knew he resembled an outlaw more than a respectable cattle rancher. A skinny, too-tall outlaw.

It couldn't be his sparkling personality that attracted women, he thought, his lips twisting into what could almost pass for a smile. Growing up the way he had, he'd never really had much opportunity to develop what he supposed folks would refer to as "social graces." And later on he'd thrown all his energies into improving his lot in life, with a single-minded determination that hadn't allowed time to learn the give and take of getting along with people.

And it definitely wasn't his flair for fashion. The western-style shirts he habitually wore made no claim whatever to sartorial splendor, and the best that could be said for the faded jeans that hung from his lean hips was that they kept him decently covered.

No, he didn't understand what it was about him that made women react in strange ways. All he could figure out was that maybe his skinny frame and taciturn manner brought out their motherly instincts. Not that he'd had much experience with mothers. His own had run out on him when he was little more than a baby, leaving him to spend his childhood and teenage years in various foster homes and institutions. Although it hadn't been the ideal way to grow up, all in all it hadn't been too bad. Until—

He shook his head, as if to rid himself of the memory.

Chapter Three

Jamie couldn't control a flutter of apprehension. This was her first trip into town since she'd gone to see Warren several days ago. That had been bad enough. She'd been able to feel the stares—some curious, but many hostile—as soon as the townsfolk began to recognize her.

Today it was even worse, since she was driving the ranch truck instead of her little compact car. That beat-up green pickup was familiar to just about everyone in town. Driving down McClintock's main street, she was aware of heads turning, of people leaning close to one another as they conducted whispered conversations.

You knew it was going to be like this, she reminded herself as she parked the truck in front of Roy Mayfield's hardware store. Although she had allowed herself to hope that maybe in time the talk would die down, she knew how unlikely that was. As Warren had said, ''. . . folks around here have long memories.'' She could picture herself years from now, a bitter old lady, still being shunned by the people she'd once considered her friends.

There was no reason why she'd *had* to come back, of course. Nobody had twisted her arm. She couldn't run a ranch long-distance, though. The only other alternative would have been to sell it, but everything in her rebelled against letting it go out of the family. Anyway, she'd stayed away too long.

She'd let herself be intimidated into leaving, but five years of being out on her own had stiffened her resolve and instilled a fierce determination in her. She'd come back to her rightful home and she wasn't going to allow anyone to drive her away again.

Having given herself this pep talk, she pushed open the heavy door and entered the hardware store.

Once inside, she nodded coolly to several customers she encountered, her impassive demeanor belying the thudding of her heart.

Cole squinted at the scrap of paper in his hand, trying to decipher Levi's scrawl. Scanning the display of pump parts, he found what he was looking for and headed for the checkout counter.

As he neared the front of the store, he slowed almost to a halt. The proprietor, Roy Mayfield, was ringing up several items for Gus Millard, and just behind Gus, a carton of fence staples in her arms, was Jamie Cantrell.

At Cole's approach, Roy glanced up. "Howdy, Cole," he said. "Be with you in a minute."

"No hurry," Cole replied. He nodded a brief, impersonal greeting to Jamie, hoping nothing in his demeanor revealed that she had been on his mind ever since that encounter in the library.

Although the usual conversation was going on among the other customers, as they discussed cattle prices or grumbled about the lack of rain, the voices were muted, cautious, as if people were expecting something out of the ordinary to happen.

As Gus pocketed his change and headed for the door with his purchases, Roy looked past Jamie as if he didn't see her. "Lessee, now—Cole, I think you were next."

At Roy's words, Cole saw Jamie's eyes widen and her mouth form a little O of surprise. Watching the emotions that played across her face, he could tell the exact moment her surprise gave way to indignation. It was evident in the flash of resentment that turned her eyes from a soft misty green to the icy glitter of emeralds, in the sudden rush of color that stained her cheeks and the slight lifting of her chin. Her angry glare included Cole as well as Roy.

Conversation near the checkout counter tapered off. Cole was aware that the other customers were watching the little tableau with interest. In the sudden silence, a multitude of thoughts ran through his mind.

It was a small incident, not worth making a big deal over, he told himself. With several customers milling around, Roy could easily have lost track of who was next to be waited on. Cole had an uneasy feeling that that wasn't the case, though. The girl had been standing right in front of him. It was obvious the slight had been intentional. *Stay out of it,* his better judgment said. Whatever Roy had against Jamie, it was between the two of them. He had no desire to get stuck in the middle of it.

He was caught off guard by the sudden rush of anger that surged through him, though. He knew how it felt to be ignored by "respectable" people, as if he didn't exist.

He fixed Roy with a steady gaze. "I believe the young lady was next," he said. Although he didn't raise his voice, there was something in the very softness of his tone that held a note of warning.

The stocky, heavily built storekeeper returned his look hostilely. Several seconds ticked by as the two men glared at one another. Roy was the first to look away. "I—ah— didn't realize Jamie was here before you, Cole." He gave a self-conscious shrug as he turned his attention to her.

"A carton of fence staples," he said, punching keys on the cash register. "That be all for you today?"

"Yes, thank you." Jamie's tone was cool and composed.

The entire incident was over so quickly that it was actually more of a "nonincident," Cole thought. Had Roy meant to ignore Jamie, or had it been an honest mistake?

It only took a few seconds for Cole to complete his own transaction. He reached the door just as Jamie was struggling to hold it open and get through it without dropping the heavy box she was carrying. He had the air of a man whose primary goal was simply to "get the show on the road," as he lifted one arm up over Jamie's head and put a hand on the door to keep it from closing. With his other hand, he reached around her to grasp the carton.

The action was automatic. With his usual no-nonsense approach to any situation, he'd determined that this was the quickest way to get himself and Jamie out of the store. He knew they were still being watched with interest by the other customers, and he just wanted to get away from all those prying eyes.

Jamie's grip on the carton tightened as her head whipped around. Still smarting over Roy's slight, she was determined to make it clear to whoever had come up behind her that she didn't need anyone's help. "I can manage—" she began, a flash of fire in her eyes. The words died on her lips as she saw that it was Cole.

He nodded for her to go through the door ahead of him.

Jamie hesitated. Her first impulse was to yank her package away from him and sweep out of the store with whatever aplomb she had left. Something in his manner told her he wasn't going to be deterred that easily, though, and she didn't want to call any more attention to herself by standing there having a tug-of-war with this tall stranger over a carton of fence staples. Besides, there was an innate dignity about him that made her feel she would be insulting him if she refused his help. Resigned, she relinquished the box to him and went out the door.

When they were on the sidewalk she turned to him. "I'll take that now."

But he ignored her outstretched hands as his gaze swept the parking area in front of the store. Spotting the green pickup, he deposited the carton in the truck bed.

There seemed to be nothing left for Jamie to say except, "Thank you."

"No problem." He touched the wide brim of his hat in a gesture that dismissed it as hardly worth mentioning.

"It's nice to know chivalry isn't completely dead," Jamie couldn't resist murmuring. If Cole heard her, he gave no indication as he turned and walked away.

What was that all about? Cole wondered as he headed down the street. He'd always known Roy Mayfield to be a decent enough guy. Why would he deliberately slight this harmless-looking woman? And the longer he mulled it over, the more convinced he was that Roy's action *had* been deliberate.

Maybe old Roy was just having a bad day, he thought with a shrug. Lord knows, the man had enough troubles that he really couldn't be blamed if once in a while he got a little testy. His only son, Randy, had been injured in a car accident several years ago and still walked with a limp.

As if that in itself wasn't enough of a burden, the son seemed to feel that, because of his injury, the precepts of civilized behavior no longer applied to him. Although Cole had little more than a nodding acquaintance with Randy Mayfield, he was aware, as was everyone else in town, that the young man drank too much, drove too fast, and generally ignored the rules to which others were expected to adhere.

Cole recalled some of Levi's remarks on the subject. "It's about time that feller got his act together," the old man had commented once, when word had gotten around that Randy had been stopped for drunken driving over in Drewsey. "He ain't a kid no more. He was supposed to take over the store so his pa could retire, but ever since that accident, he seems bent on driving pore ol' Roy into an early grave.

" 'Course, he warn't all that much of a bargain even before that," he went on, after a moment's thought. "Always was kinda wild. Seemed to have a way with the young ladies in town, though. Must've been them dark eyes and that thick curly hair. And it didn't hurt none that he was the big football star back in high school. 'Spect he broke a lotta girls' hearts when he married that Palmer girl."

Now fragments of that conversation came back to Cole. What was it Levi had said? ". . . When he married that Palmer girl . . ." Much of the old man's gossipy ramblings went right over Cole's head, but now something nagged at the edges of his consciousness, some connection that he couldn't quite place. The only Palmers he recalled were Frank and Nadine.

Of course—it came back to him now. Their daughter Sheila was married to Randy. And Sheila would be Jamie's cousin. But that still didn't explain Roy's deliberate slight to Jamie.

Warren Eagleton had admitted, the last time Cole talked to him, that there was ''no love lost between Jamie and the Palmers . . .'' Whatever that was supposed to mean. It didn't explain Roy's attitude.

Maybe he shouldn't have interfered in the incident back in the store, Cole thought. He wouldn't have, if he hadn't found himself right in the middle of it. Opening a door or carrying a heavy package for Jamie was one thing, but he had no desire to get caught up in someone else's family feud.

Jamie stared after the man's retreating back—Cole, Roy had called him. He was the same person she'd bumped into in the library, of course. He must be fairly new around here—she didn't recall ever having seen him before she went away.

She had mixed emotions about his speaking up in her behalf when Roy had looked right past her. She was perfectly capable of standing up for her own rights. The only reason she hadn't was because she'd been momentarily caught off guard. She hadn't thought Roy would carry a grudge this long. After all, she'd almost become his daughter-in-law—way back in what seemed almost another life.

The point was, she didn't want anyone running interference for her. When she'd made the decision to return to McClintock, she'd known there would be some rough times ahead, that there would be people who would shun her. But this was her town—her home—and she'd made up her mind that she wasn't going to hang her head in shame, or behave as if she had no right to be here.

She supposed this—this Cole Wyatt had meant well. The last thing she needed, though, was a knight in shining armor leaping to her defense any time her rights were in danger of being violated. She didn't want to be beholden to anyone, even in such a small matter.

Of course, she reminded herself, once the town gossips got to him, he wouldn't be so quick to get involved.

By now Jamie just wanted to get back to the ranch before anything else embarrassing happened, but she'd told Warren she'd stop by his office. He'd called and said there was some paperwork that needed to be taken care of. Might as well get that over with, she thought. Then she wouldn't have to make another trip into town for a week or two.

"Jamie, good to see you," Warren welcomed her warmly. As he ushered her into his office, he told his secretary, "Evelyn, would you get those papers for Jamie to sign?"

"Now then," he said, closing the door behind them, "how's everything going out at the ranch?"

"Pretty well, all things considered. TJ says he's glad I'm planning to keep the ranch—that he didn't like the idea of the place being sold to strangers. And the other men who've agreed to stay seem to be satisfied with their decision. I don't know if they're doing it for me or out of loyalty to my folks, but they're a good crew, and I'm lucky to have them. Of course, we've still had to hire a couple of new hands."

"I admire your determination to stick it out," Warren said. "I have to admit I thought you were making a big mistake when you said you were going to run the ranch yourself, but I have a feeling you're going to make it. I guess selling the place would have been the easy way out, especially with a qualified buyer ready to take over.

"By the way, who was it that made the offer?" Jamie asked.

"Name's Cole Wyatt. He bought the old Lucky Horseshoe spread. Tall fellow, doesn't smile much. You'll be running into him one of these days."

"I already did, the other day in the library," Jamie replied. "Literally."

Warren's eyebrows raised in a questioning expression.

"I was hurrying around a corner and I ran smack into him," Jamie explained. "I nearly knocked him down." She hesitated before going on, then decided she might as well tell him about the encounter in the hardware store too. If she didn't, someone else would be sure to.

With a shrug, as if to downplay the whole thing as much possible, she related the incident at Mayfield's—including the way Cole had spoken up in her defense. "He didn't make a big deal out of it, or even raise his voice," she finished up, "but Roy seemed a little shamefaced over his behavior."

Warren grinned. "By golly, I wish I'd been there to see that." Then his manner turned serious. "Jamie, I'm afraid you're going to have to face this sort of thing a lot. Other folks aren't going to be any more forgiving."

Jamie sighed. "I thought I was prepared for this, but it hurts to be treated that way by people I've known all my life."

"Why don't you just tell folks the truth about what happened that night?"

"They didn't believe me five years ago," she pointed out. "There's no reason to think they would now."

"I suppose you're right. They've made up their minds. But things never should have gotten to this point. When it first happened, you should have *insisted* people listen to your side of the story."

"I was in no condition to insist on anything," Jamie reminded him. "Don't forget, I was unconscious when I was pulled out of that car. By the time I was able to tell my side of the story, nobody believed me except my parents—and you and Marianne, of course, and a few others. Most folks had already formed their opinions.''

''With a little help from Sheila.'' Warren's voice held a note of contempt. ''She was playing her role as the 'wronged wife' to the hilt.'' His tone became thoughtful. ''I always wondered how she happened to come on the scene so soon.''

''There's no point in dwelling on what happened in the past,'' Jamie said matter-of-factly. ''It's over and done with, and rehashing it isn't going to change anything. Now then, are those papers ready for me to sign?''

Cole was on his way out of town when he remembered he'd planned to stop by Warren's office before he returned home. He still hadn't gotten an answer about whether Jamie intended to accept his offer on the Circle C, and Levi had been nagging him about it all week.

''Go on over and talk to her,'' the old man had kept saying.

''I can't do that,'' Cole had protested. ''It'd look like I'm rushing her. I'll wait until I hear from Warren.''

''Don't know why you're dragging your feet about this,'' Levi muttered. ''A body'd think you're scared of her. Little thing like that ain't gonna bite your head off.''

''I'd rather do business with Warren,'' Cole had insisted. Finally, in order to pacify Levi, he'd said he'd go see Warren the next time he was in town. He'd better do that before heading back to the ranch. If he didn't, he'd never hear the end of it from Levi.

He'd never hear the end of it anyway, he thought as he made a U-turn at the end of McClintock's main street, if Levi knew he'd come face to face with Jamie a couple of times, and had passed up the opportunity to mention his

offer to her. Somehow, neither encounter had seemed quite
the right time to bring up the subject.

"Cole, come in." Warren greeted him with a hearty
handshake. "What can I do for you?"

"I was in town, so I thought I'd stop by and see if you'd
had a chance to talk to Jamie Cantrell—about whether
she's interested in selling her ranch."

"As a matter of fact, I've been meaning to give you a
call, but I just haven't gotten around to it." He paused,
looking slightly uncomfortable.

As Cole waited for him to go on, he had a feeling whatever Warren had to say wasn't going to be what he wanted
to hear. Warren's next words proved him right.

"I'm sorry to tell you—she's turned down your offer."

Cole felt a stab of disappointment. "You mean someone
else came up with a better one?"

"No, it's not that. She's decided she wants to keep the
place."

"Keep it?" Cole echoed, surprised. "I didn't think she
had any interest in running the place herself."

"Ah—I'm afraid it was my fault you got the wrong idea.
I just assumed she'd want to sell out. Not that I wouldn't
like to see her stay, but—well, she's going to have a rough
time. Folks around here can be pretty narrow-minded."

Well, that was that, Cole thought. As he turned to leave,
Warren's voice followed him. "You just missed her, you
know. She left here just a few moments ago. I wish you'd
come by a little sooner so I could have introduced you—
although I understand you did meet, more or less, a little
earlier."

Since Cole had no idea whether Warren was referring to
the collision in the library or the incident in the hardware

store, he simply lifted one shoulder in a noncommittal shrug.

"Now that she's decided to stay here, she's going to be your closest neighbor," Warren pointed out. He paused briefly, before going on. "You were good friends with her parents. I hope you will be with Jamie, too. She's going to need all the friends she can get."

Cole wasn't sure how to reply to this. He'd already gathered that Jamie was in disfavor with the good people of McClintock. Although he couldn't suppress a mild curiosity as to exactly what she'd done, he reminded himself the less he knew about Jamie Cantrell and her problems, the better off he'd be. He saw no reason to change his policy of keeping out of other people's private affairs. True, he'd been on friendly terms with Jamie's parents, but they hadn't intruded on his privacy, nor he on theirs.

As he drove home a little later, he had the uneasy feeling that there were going to be some changes in his peaceful, well-ordered life that he wasn't going to be happy with. It seemed that Warren was expecting him to befriend Jamie, to help her ease her way back into the good graces of the community, and the whole idea filled him with dismay.

Chapter Four

Cole tossed another bale of hay onto the stack with such force that a cloud of dust puffed out around it.

He'd learned from experience that vigorous physical activity was the most effective method of working off his frustration when his plans didn't go the way he'd hoped. Taking his disappointment out on inanimate objects—like hay bales—was preferable to allowing it to eat away at him.

And it was no use pretending he *wasn't* disappointed. He'd counted on enlarging his ranch with the addition of the Circle C. There wasn't even anyone he could blame because things hadn't worked out. If Jamie Cantrell chose not to sell, that was her privilege.

"Hey Boss, you in there?" Levi's raspy voice reached Cole, as a shadow fell across the open door of the barn.

Cole groaned inwardly. He was in no mood to discuss his failed plans. It had to come out into the open sometime, though, he reminded himself. "Over here," he called.

Levi ambled over to where Cole was working and stood with his hands in his pockets, surveying the fast-growing stack of hay. "You're working like the devil hisself was after you. There ain't no big rush, you know."

"Might as well get it done now, instead of waiting until the last minute," Cole muttered. He worked in silence for a while, aware that Levi was watching his every move. Finally, when he paused to wipe a forearm across his brow, he asked, "Something on your mind?"

"I been thinking about some of the changes we can make around here when you buy the Circle C. We can start by irrigating that section down by the—"

"I won't be buying the Circle C." Cole swung another bale into place. "I talked to Warren when I was in town. He said the Cantrell woman has decided to keep it."

Levi's weather-beaten face crinkled into a smile of satisfaction. "Well now, I'm mighty pleased to hear it."

Cole shot him a look of surprise. "I thought you were all fired up for me to buy the Cantrell ranch."

"If it was going up for sale I'd rather you bought it than have it go into strange hands. The Cantrells have been neighbors for as long as I've worked here, and I didn't cotton to the idea of strangers taking over the place. I'm relieved to know Jamie'll be staying on. I know you and her'll get to be real good friends."

Cole didn't share Levi's enthusiasm. It was bad enough that Eagleton had hinted that he hoped Cole would become some sort of "protector" to Jamie. And now Levi was expecting him to be "real good friends" with her. He had a feeling his zealously guarded privacy was about to be invaded.

"Yes sir, I'm mighty pleased," Levi went on. "I've known Jamie since she was just a mite of a thing, and she's a fine little gal. I never did believe all that stuff about her and Randy Mayfield. Oh, I know Randy was in Jamie's car with her when that accident happened, but there was likely some good reason why they was together.''

Cole knew if he displayed the least bit of curiosity about the accident Levi was referring to, he'd end up hearing more about Jamie's past than he ever wanted to. The only way to discourage the old man's gabbiness was to ignore it. Grabbing another bale, he hardened his features into a stern expression that—he hoped—made it clear that as far as he was concerned, the subject was closed.

''Now I've got you,'' Jamie muttered under her breath to the half dozen stray cows she'd been chasing for the better part of an hour. ''Stupid animals.'' She remembered once hearing an old, experienced cowhand make the statement that range cattle had the ''IQ of a fence post.'' *Truer words were never spoken,* she thought now.

These particular cows weren't even hers. While she was up on the east ridge this morning, she'd spotted them making their way through a break in the fence that ran across the property line between her ranch and the Lucky Horseshoe.

There had been a long-standing agreement that since this section of fence bordered the Lucky Horseshoe's upper pasture, their crew would maintain it. Jamie had expected her new neighbor to honor that agreement. Apparently, he wasn't doing so. She felt a flash of irritation.

She wasn't in the best of moods today anyway. She was putting in some exceptionally long hours lately. Two of the new hands TJ had hired to replace the men who'd quit were young and inexperienced, and until they learned the ropes, everyone had to put in extra hours.

She supposed she could just call Cole and tell him, ''Some of your cattle got through the fence and are running all over my land. Please come after them—and get that fence repaired.'' She'd felt vaguely beholden to Cole ever since he'd come to her defense in the hardware store, though, even though she'd tried to tell herself he'd simply reacted automatically, out of common courtesy. Having resolved to prove to everyone around here that she could manage quite well on her own, she was reluctant to accept favors, even small ones. By rounding up Cole's strays and holding them for him, score.

She'd finally managed to drive the elusive cattle into a shallow ravine, where they were hemmed in on three sides. Now all she had to do was get them headed in the right direction and herd them into a holding pen.

One of the cows—the largest and most aggressive—eyed her cautiously, as if sensing her intentions. Jamie glared back at him. *The IQ of a fence post,* she reminded herself. Surely she ought to be able to outsmart a cow.

With a surprising agility, the beast suddenly broke to the right. As if that was the signal they had been waiting for, the other cows followed his lead, scattering in six different directions.

By the time the cows finally tired of the game, and were docilely heading down the hill toward the holding pen, Jamie could feel little beads of perspiration running down between her shoulder blades. Her shirt was plastered to her back and her hair had escaped the strip of cloth that held it back, and was in disarray around her face. She was hot and sticky and tired.

And it was all Cole Wyatt's fault, for not having that fence repaired.

She had intended to call him when she got back to the house and politely inform him that some of his cows had gotten loose and she was holding them for him. But by the time she maneuvered the last of them into the pen and closed the gate securely, she was no longer in a "polite" frame of mind. Having just spent most of the morning chasing after *his* strays, she felt that whatever small debt she owed him for standing up for her in the hardware store had been more than repaid. *We're even now, Mr. Wyatt,* she thought.

Maybe her dad had been easygoing about that sort of thing—Trace Cantrell had always been inclined to overlook other people's shortcomings—but Cole wasn't dealing with her dad now. She might as well make it clear to him right from the beginning that she had no intention of being as lenient as her father. She had enough problems without having to contend with a neighbor who was too shiftless or irresponsible to keep his fences in good repair.

That meant paying him a visit. Although she hated to take time out of her busy schedule to call on him, she felt it was important to confront him face to face, just to make sure he understood what a serious matter this was.

Taking time only to unsaddle her horse and give him a quick rubdown, and grab the keys to the pickup, she was soon on her way to the Wyatt ranch. She wanted to have this out with Cole while her anger was still at its height.

"All I'm saying is that it ain't right for a man not to be on friendly terms with his neighbors." Bending over the rusty old tractor, Levi frowned in concentration as he peered at the innards of the machine. He wiggled a few wires experimentally. "Hand me that screwdriver."

Cole placed the screwdriver in Levi's outstretched hand. "And all *I'm* saying is that she probably doesn't want people butting into her business." He was getting tired of the argument, which had been going on for a week or so, ever since Levi had learned that Jamie was planning to stay on and run the ranch herself.

"It wouldn't hurt to stop by and say 'Hey,' just to sort of welcome her back home," Levi had suggested at first. When that failed to get a response from Cole, he casually mentioned, "One of the boys from the Circle C was telling me their hay baler's broke down. You might go over and offer her the use of ours so she can get her hay in."

But Cole had stubbornly shied away from any contact, business or otherwise, with his neighbor. "I'm *not* going over to see Jamie Cantrell. I don't even know her."

"And you ain't never going to if you keep acting so standoffish," Levi predicted, shaking his head in annoyance.

That suited Cole just fine, but he refrained from saying so. Anyway, in the back of his mind he knew it wasn't just the threat to his privacy that was making him reluctant to have anything to do with Jamie. It went deeper than that. The memory of how soft and warm she'd felt in his arms, of the fresh scent of her hair, stirred feelings that could only lead to trouble. . . .

He pushed the disturbing thoughts away.

"We ain't gonna be needing the baler for a while," Levi reminded him, as he tinkered with the tractor. "Somebody might as well be getting some use out of it."

It didn't appear that he was going to drop the subject. He was going to keep harping on this until Cole came around to his way of thinking. What was more, it was working.

Already a vague sense of guilt was nagging at Cole. After all, he'd had a good working relationship with Jamie's parents. They'd often shared equipment or labor. He supposed it wouldn't hurt him to unbend a little and let Jamie know he was willing to continue the arrangement.

True, offering any assistance at all would mean emerging from his protective armor of reserve just a little. He reminded himself, however, that whatever contact he had with Jamie would be nothing more than a business relationship. It was unlikely that extending a little neighborly courtesy was going to seriously jeopardize his privacy.

He lifted one shoulder in a casual shrug. "She's welcome to the use of our baler, if you want to make the offer. I don't have time."

"The offer oughta come from you. After all, you're the boss around here."

"Nice of you to admit it," Cole muttered.

"What's that?"

"Nothing. How're you coming with the tractor?"

"Let's give it a try. Start 'er up."

The engine reluctantly sputtered to life as Cole pressed the starter button.

"You might even send a couple of our boys over to give her a hand. I know they're kinda short-handed right now." Levi's words were almost drowned out by the fitful chugging of the engine.

Cole was getting a little tired of being pushed. "All right, if it'll make you happy, I'll offer her the use of our hay baler. And I'll send a couple of our hands along. I'll send her the whole crew," he said irritably. "Do you think maybe we ought to give her half our herd too?"

Levi gave him a look of offended dignity. "I dunno what you're getting so riled up about. I just thought it wouldn't hurt to show a little neighborly friendliness."

Cole felt a twinge of regret for his surly attitude. He knew the old man meant well. "Sorry," he muttered. Apologies didn't come easily to him.

Levi turned his attention back to the tractor. He made an adjustment or two, and it began to run more smoothly. "Wouldn't hurt to put in a new set of plugs," he commented, handing the screwdriver back to Cole. He pulled a rag from his hip pocket and wiped his hands with it. "Well, what do you think?"

"About the tractor? Oh—it sounds better."

Levi gave him a withering look. "About Jamie."

Cole drew a resigned sigh. "You win. I'll drop by her place tomorrow and see if she wants to use our baler."

"You don't need to make it sound like you're going to a hanging. Jamie's about as nice a young woman as you'd ever want to meet. . . ."

Levi's words trailed off as he and Cole both turned to stare at the pickup truck coming down the gravel road toward the ranch. It was approaching at such a high rate of speed that it was almost obliterated by the clouds of dust swirling up around it.

"Speak of the devil," Levi mumbled under his breath.

Both men winced as the truck squealed into the driveway and came to a screeching halt, sending gravel spewing out from beneath the tires. Levi and Cole stared in open-mouthed surprise as the door flew open and Jamie got out. As she stood with her hands on her hips, glaring at them, it was obvious she was extremely displeased about something.

Despite Cole's certainty that an unpleasant scene was about to take place, it crossed his mind, briefly, that she looked especially attractive with that high color in her cheeks, and sparks shooting from her eyes. And it didn't escape his notice that her lightweight shirt and denim jeans outlined every curve of her slender body in a way that stirred something deep inside him.

Levi was the first to find his voice. "Lord, girl, you look like you been rode hard and put away wet."

"Would you like to know *why* I look this way?" Her voice was soft, disarming, but beneath her courteous words was an undertone of controlled anger.

The two men exchanged glances. From their twin expressions it was obvious that neither of them would be so foolhardy as to hazard a guess.

"I'll *tell* you why." Jamie marched up to Cole and confronted him squarely, tilting her head back so she could look into his face. "I've just spent the past couple of hours rounding up *your* strays. Because *somebody*—" Her tone left no doubt as to who that somebody might be. "—didn't repair that fence up on the east ridge. There's a gap in it big enough for your entire herd to get through. In fact, they probably have by now, and are running all over my range."

Cole sent Levi a look that clearly said the older man had missed the mark in his assessment of Jamie. If she was his idea of ". . . as nice a young woman as you'd ever want to meet . . ." Levi must be getting senile.

"People who don't have enough respect for their neighbors to keep their fence lines in good repair shouldn't be allowed to be in the ranching business," she went on.

As Jamie's tirade continued, Cole's mouth tightened grimly and his expression became a stony mask. Noticing this, her air of righteous indignation wavered just a bit, until she reminded herself that *he* was the one who was in the wrong. She had no intention of letting him intimidate her with that steely glare. "In ranch country there's no excuse for that kind of carelessness," she said coldly.

"Ah, begging your pardon, ma'am," Levi put in, in a placating tone, "but there's something you need to know about this situation."

She shot him a cold look. "What I *know* is that it's downright criminal to let a fence get into that condition."

"Things have changed since you've been gone. Your pa leased that section of land up on the ridge from Cole. Part of the deal was that the Circle C would maintain the fence. TJ didn't tell you?"

Cole watched the changing emotions that played over Jamie's face, from anger through the dawning realization that she was the one at fault, to embarrassment. This last was obvious from the flush that rose all the way to the roots of her hair.

He had expected to experience a satisfactory sense of vindication at seeing her so effectively put in her place. Instead, all he felt was a sort of emptiness.

"N—no, he didn't mention it," she admitted.

"Guess it musta slipped his mind," Levi said charitably. "I'm surprised he let that get by him. He's one of the best ranch foremen in the county. He's usually right on top of everything."

"We—ah—we've got a couple of new men. Some of the regulars quit after—after my parents died. TJ had to take whoever he could get. I guess they didn't get the word—" Her voice trailed off, as if she realized that this was no excuse for storming over here, making unfounded accusations against her new neighbor.

"Shoot, Jamie, you been away a long time," Levi said, coming to her rescue. "You can't be expected to know all the changes that have been made."

"All the same, I had no right to jump to conclusions that way. I—I'm sorry," she apologized lamely.

"I'll send someone over after my cattle," Cole said, his tone icy. "And I'll see that the fence is repaired."

"No, it's my responsibility, and I'll handle it," Jamie insisted. "I'll hold your cattle until it's fixed, and then I'll have a couple of our hands bring them back." Struggling to maintain some semblance of dignity, she nodded a good-bye and climbed back into her pickup.

As the two men watched her drive away, Levi said, "I hope this ain't gonna have a real bad effect on yore opinion of Jamie."

"It's not likely to do it a whole lot of good," Cole muttered.

Jamie berated herself all the way home. She could hardly believe she'd been so foolish as to storm over to her new neighbor's and accuse him of all sorts of irresponsible behavior. If she hadn't had so much on her mind . . .

Ever since she'd gotten back, there had been so many demands on her time. Oh, TJ and his crew had done the best they could to keep things running smoothly until her return, but there had been some decisions that TJ simply hadn't had the authority to make. She felt she was being pulled in a dozen different directions. Between that and contending with the obvious hostility of some of the townsfolk—like Roy Mayfield—well, she wasn't thinking clearly right now. And finding her neighbor's cattle running loose on her property had been the final straw.

Still, that was no reason for her to behave the way she had. When she'd launched into her tirade she thought she'd caught a glimpse of hurt in Cole's eyes—almost as if he'd been struck. It had disappeared before she could be sure, though, to be replaced by an expression of steely hardness. Having been on the receiving end of unjust accusations herself, she was uncomfortably aware that words could be just as painful as physical blows.

She supposed she'd pretty well ruled out any possibility of the amicable relations that were so important between neighboring ranchers. After her little performance today, the best that could be hoped for now was a guarded truce. The thought sent an unexpected pang of regret through her. Because of her thoughtless words, she had effectively alienated one of the few people she might possibly have counted on as an ally.

And although she was reluctant to admit it, even to herself, she could use a friend.

Chapter Five

"Jamie," Val's voice came over the phone, "I just made a big pot of soup, and I thought I'd bring you some."

"Oh, Val, that's so thoughtful of you."

"Hey, it's nothing, really. The way the guys in my family eat, I always feel like I'm cooking for an army anyway. I'll be over in a little while."

While Jamie talked to Val, she was stretching an arm around behind her, in an attempt to reach that spot in the middle of her back that needed to be scratched. She'd been working in the hay field all morning, and she itched all over from the little particles of hay that had worked their way down inside her clothes.

Despite her discomfort, there was a sense of relief in knowing the hay was safely cut, baled, and stacked under cover. With her baler needing repairs, she'd realized she could easily lose the entire crop if a rainstorm came up. While the loss of one cutting might not be a major disaster, it would still amount to more than a slight setback. Like

45

the other ranchers in the area, she depended on the hay crop to nourish her herd through the winter months.

Now, thanks to Cole Wyatt's generosity—or, more likely, Levi's—her hay was in and she could take a breathing spell before the next emergency came up.

But right now the first order of business was to get out of these scratchy clothes and into the shower.

"Don't it give you a good feeling to do a neighborly turn for someone?" Levi asked as he maneuvered the pickup around the potholes in the dirt road between the Lucky Horseshoe and the Circle C.

"Not especially," Cole, riding in the passenger seat, replied in clipped tones. "I was already feeling okay."

"Mebbe so," Levi said, undaunted by his employer's lack of enthusiasm, "but there's nothing like doing something nice for someone else to put a person in a good mood."

As if to contradict Levi's words, Cole scowled darkly. It wasn't that he minded lending a hand—or a piece of equipment—to someone who needed it. That sort of thing was common practice among neighboring ranchers. He just wished Levi wouldn't make such a big deal out of the whole thing.

Earlier today, when he was out looking over the barn with a critical eye, thinking it could use a new coat of paint, Levi had driven up next to him in the pickup, and called out the window, "Hey boss, you doing anything in partik'ler?"

"Not at the moment. Why?"

"Why don't you hop in? I'm headed into town to see if them parts came in for the generator. I can drop you off at the Cantrell place so you can bring the baler back. I ran into TJ, and he says they're done with it."

"What's the hurry? I'm sure they'll get it back to us by the time we're ready for it."

"I'm going right by there, and you just said you ain't doing nothing real important right now. Like you always say, there's no sense in putting off a job till the last minute."

"I never—" Cole began, but his words trailed off as he recalled, with chagrin, having said something to that effect just the other day. With a resigned sigh, he got into the truck.

Although he told himself he had more important matters to attend to, he knew that wasn't the real reason he was so reluctant to go over to the Cantrell ranch.

Ever since that day when Jamie had unexpectedly ended up in his arms, the memory had dominated more of his waking hours than he cared to admit. Despite his best efforts to put her out of his mind, his senses wouldn't let him forget how small and fragile she'd felt in his embrace. Thoughts of the way she'd fit so nicely in his arms penetrated into his consciousness when he was least expecting it.

His common sense told him the smartest thing he could do would be to stay as far away from Jamie Cantrell as possible.

There was nobody around when Levi dropped him off at the Cantrell place. When his tentative, "Hello?" elicited no response, he walked through the barn, then checked the other outbuildings. Although the baler, still hitched to the tractor, was in plain sight in the lean-to behind the barn, he felt he ought to let somebody know he was taking it. Reluctantly, he headed toward the house.

As he rapped on the back door, it swung inward. He wasn't too surprised, since people around here seldom locked their houses. It wouldn't have seemed neighborly otherwise. Hesitantly, he pushed the door open a little wider and glanced into the kitchen. There was nobody in sight, but he could hear the sound of movement in another part of the house.

"Jamie?" he called out.

When there was no answer, he shifted his weight from one foot to the other as he considered what to do next. In this rural area, where anyone within a forty-mile radius was considered a close neighbor, people didn't stand on ceremony. It was common practice for a visitor to open the door of someone's house, or even step inside, and call out something like, "Hey, anybody home?" He had occasionally done so himself, when dropping by to see Jamie's father. And Trace Cantrell had done the same at Cole's house.

But things were different now. The easygoing friendship he'd had with his late neighbor was a far cry from the guarded wariness that existed between himself and the new owner of the Cantrell ranch.

Although his instinct urged him to make a hasty retreat, he felt that if he left without at least making his presence known, it might look as if he were nursing a grudge over that matter of the fence repairs. He had to admit, he *was* still smarting a little over the way Jamie had automatically jumped to the conclusion that he was the one at fault. He'd made up his mind to not make an issue of it, though.

"Jamie?" he called again. Listening intently, he heard what could have been a door opening and closing.

She *was* home. He hadn't realized he'd been subconsciously hoping she wouldn't be. It was too late to back out now, though. He couldn't just turn around and leave without letting her know he'd been here.

Steadying the half open door, he knocked on it again, more loudly this time. After a moment's silence, Jamie's

"Come on in—I'm in here," drifted out to him. *Might as well get this over with,* he thought, as he followed the sound of her voice.

A few long strides took him into the living room. He'd state his business in a succinct, matter-of-fact manner, then get out of there as quickly as possible. But when Jamie entered from a doorway on the opposite side of the room, his carefully rehearsed little speech deserted him.

She was clad in a thick white bathrobe that came almost all the way to the floor. Obviously unaware of his presence, she was bending forward with her head down, vigorously rubbing her hair with towel. As she took a few steps into the room a faint, flowery scent seemed to surround her. Straightening, she tossed her head back.

He knew he ought to say something to let her know he was there, but she made such an attractive picture, with her upraised arms emphasizing her slender form, that for a few seconds he could do nothing but stare, speechless. It occurred to him that if she was going to be running around the house in her robe, she shouldn't be calling out, "Come in," to just anyone, without knowing who was at the door.

In the few seconds before she realized he was there, Cole had time to notice the soft pink flush that adorned her cheeks, and the way her pale golden hair settled around her face in tousled waves.

She looked so utterly appealing that he ached to take her in his arms, to breathe in that sweet, fresh scent . . .

Her large expressive eyes became suddenly wider and her lips parted in stunned surprise as she spotted Cole. She emitted a little startled exclamation.

All at once he was jolted out of his trance. "I—I'm sorry—" he got out. "The back door was open . . . I knocked, and I—I thought I heard you say come in. I must have been mistaken."

''No, you—ah—weren't mistaken. I—I was expecting someone else.''

Who? Cole almost blurted out. He suppressed the sudden stab of jealousy that surged through him. ''Just the same, I should have made sure you knew it was me.''

Jamie pulled a deep breath into her lungs, trying to calm her erratically racing pulse and heartbeat. The sight of Cole Wyatt standing in her living room, tall and lean-hipped, the brim of his Stetson shading his face, had been unnerving, to say the least. She was expecting Val, of course, when she'd heard the knock just as she was getting out of the shower.

Don't make a big deal out of this, she told herself. After all, he wasn't some intruder who'd violated her privacy. She *had* called out for him to come in. Knowing the casual way things were done around here, she shouldn't have just assumed it was Val who had knocked. It could have been anyone—TJ, or one of the hands.

It occurred to her, belatedly, to wonder *why* he was here. She was quite sure this wasn't a social call. She wished he would simply state his business and leave. She couldn't deny that his presence was disconcerting. She wasn't sure what it was about him; his exceptional height, maybe, or that air of power which seemed to be a part of him—and of which he seemed totally unaware—but something was sending a tingling weakness through her entire body.

A little voice inside her told her it could be because she'd caught a flash of something—admiration, perhaps—in his eyes, just before he'd covered it up with an impassive, impersonal expression.

This is ridiculous, she thought. A person would think she'd never been alone with a man before. Still, her common sense warned her it might be a good idea to get to the business at hand and get him out of here—before he became aware of the effect he was having on her.

"You wanted to see me about something?" she prompted.

"I—ah—just came by to pick up the baler . . ." He sounded distracted. "If you're finished with it, that is."

"Yes I—I am." She was dismayed at the shakiness in her voice. It was hard to maintain her composure with him towering over her that way. Automatically, she took a few steps backwards, until she came up against the wall behind her. "I was going to have one of the men return it, but as long as you're here . . ." She gave a little shrug, as if to indicate it really didn't matter much one way or the other.

"Well—ah—I'll be on my way, then." He made no move to leave, however.

As the silence between them lengthened, Jamie recalled the expression in his eyes a few moments earlier. She couldn't deny feeling a little thrill over the knowledge that Cole had found her appealing.

She tried to stifle it. Why should it matter to her that he liked her looks? She told herself it was nothing but plain old feminine vanity. Didn't every woman enjoy knowing she was considered attractive? The fact that Cole was the one who found her so was irrelevant. It certainly wasn't as if he were someone she was interested in romantically. Still, she couldn't shut out the memory of the unexpected glow that warmed her from head to toe when she'd recognized that gleam in his eyes.

With a start, she realized the turn her thoughts were taking. A primitive warning sounded in the back of her mind. It wasn't Cole she was afraid of, though, but her own suddenly chaotic emotions.

She tried to think of something trite and conventional to say, something that would break this spell and put things back into their proper perspective. But her throat felt dry, and she found herself unable to utter a word.

She wasn't sure which of them had moved, but they seemed to be separated by a scant few feet. He was close enough that she could have reached out and run her fingers along the rugged lines of his face . . .

This wouldn't do. "Thanks for the loan of the baler," she said, hoping she sounded more composed than she felt.

"No problem. I knew you'd want to get your hay in, in case it rains . . ."

His words trailed off, as if he were having trouble concentrating on the matter at hand. Hesitantly, Jamie raised her eyes to his. What she saw in his gaze sent a tingle of excitement through her. "Yes, I—I wouldn't want my crop to be ruined."

All at once she was intensely aware of his closeness, of the masculine aromas of leather and some tangy aftershave that emanated from him.

"No—of course not." His voice was warm and husky. "Be a shame to lose your hay."

Jamie nodded wordlessly. She allowed her glance to wander over the strong contours of his face, stopping at the firm lines of his mouth—wondering how his lips would feel on hers . . .

"Jamie—are you there?"

The spell was broken. "In here," Jamie replied, feeling as if she'd just been pulled back from the edge of a cliff.

"I put the soup on the stove." Val's voice drifted in from the kitchen. "I brought enough so you could get a couple of meals out of . . ."

She left the sentence dangling as she came into the living room. Her surprised glance darted from Jamie, in her unusual attire, to Cole, and back to Jamie. The only indication that she sensed the tension in the room was the barely perceptible lifting of her eyebrows.

Cole was the first to recover his equilibrium. He nodded a greeting to Val and touched the brim of his hat. " 'Afternoon, ma'am," he said, backing away from Jamie.

"Nice to see you, Cole," Val responded.

Jamie made an effort to pull her scattered wits together. "Cole just came to—ah—to get the hay baler—"

"I came for the hay baler—" Cole said at the same time.

"Ours is broken, you know," Jamie explained, her words coming out in a rush. She was surprised at how breathless her voice sounded, as if she'd been running—or as if she'd just been rescued from some unseen danger. "Cole was kind enough to let us use his. And we—we were just discussing—" All at once her mind drew a blank. What *had* they been talking about—before she'd gotten lost in Cole's gaze? Before his closeness had sent her emotions spinning?

"The weather," Cole supplied.

"Yes, the weather." Jamie shot him a grateful look.

"And—ah—hay."

"Hay—yes," Jamie murmured.

"Of course." Val's glance, as it swept over the two of them, spoke volumes.

This is not what you think, Jamie wanted to insist, but she knew that would only make matters worse. "Thanks for bringing me the soup," she said, hoping to divert Val's attention from—well, from whatever she was reading into the situation.

"Oh, I was glad to do it. There's enough for two, you know. Why not invite Cole to share it with you?"

Horrified at Val's words, Jamie attempted to catch her eye, but Val had turned to Cole. Jamie cringed as she heard

Val say to him, "I don't imagine you enjoy eating your own cooking all the time, any more than Jamie does."

Jamie could feel her cheeks burning as she tried to think of some means of extricating herself—and Cole—from this embarrassing situation. "I—I'm sure Cole has important things to do," she managed to get out.

"That's right," he confirmed hastily. "I have to—to—to get back to the ranch and—ah—start painting the barn."

"Oh. Of course. Painting the barn isn't something that can be put off," Val said.

Jamie shot her a look. Although Val's tone and manner were quite serious, Jamie detected a tiny smile playing around the corners of her mouth.

"I'll—ah—just be on my way then." Eyeing both women with a wary expression, Cole edged his way past Val and hurried from the room.

As soon as they heard the back door open and close, Val turned to Jamie. "When did you start receiving callers in your bathrobe?" she asked, wiggling her eyebrows up and down suggestively. "That's pretty racy stuff for Mc-Clintock."

"I thought it was you when I called for him to come in," Jamie replied, a spot of color staining her cheeks. "And what in the *world* were you thinking of, suggesting I invite him to stay and eat!"

Val lifted one shoulder in a casual, offhanded shrug. "You're single and unattached. He's single and unattached. What's the big deal? Sharing a pot of soup with him isn't exactly the same as choosing a silverware pattern. Why eat alone when you could be enjoying the company of your tall, lean, handsome neighbor? If I weren't a respectably married woman, I might be tempted to make a play for him myself."

"Val!" Jamie exclaimed, although she wasn't as

shocked as her tone would indicate. She knew TJ had been the only man for Val, ever since she'd fallen in love with him in high school.

"Come on," Val said. "You can't pretend you haven't noticed that the man's doggoned attractive."

Jamie could think of no suitable reply, since Cole's attributes *hadn't* escaped her notice.

"And what makes him even more so," Val went on, "is that he hasn't a clue as to the effect he has on women."

That was certainly true—or else he was putting on an awfully good act, Jamie thought. She decided she would rather not pursue the matter with Val, though. Considering the turn this conversation was taking, she thought it might be a good idea to steer the talk in another direction. She knew, however, that if she suddenly introduced an abrupt change of subject, Val would sense her reluctance to discuss Cole's appeal to women. Better to back away gradually.

"How did this Cole Wyatt come to be owner of the Lucky Horseshoe, anyway?" she asked. That seemed a safe enough topic. Besides, she was genuinely curious. "When I went away it belonged to Tom Myers."

"Tom had to put the ranch up for sale when his heart started acting up. Everybody expected that somebody around here would buy the place, but the next thing we knew Cole was the owner."

"Where did he come from?" Jamie asked.

Val shrugged. "Who knows?"

"You mean he just appeared out of nowhere, like some kind of mystery man?"

"Oh, it was nothing that dramatic. I think something was mentioned about him being from up around Seattle, but he doesn't say much about where he lived or what he did before he came here. Keeps to himself mostly."

That was unusual, Jamie thought, in this area, where everyone's life was an open book. Was he hiding something?

But that wasn't fair, she had to admit. Just because he liked to keep his private affairs private, that wasn't necessarily suspect. She recalled that during those years she'd been away, she'd shied away from forming any close friendships or talking about her past. It wasn't that she felt she had anything to hide—she knew she'd done nothing to be ashamed of. She just didn't think the details of her life were anyone else's business.

Still, she knew the people Cole had to live near and do business with might be a little suspicious of a man who was too close-mouthed. "How do the other ranchers feel about him?" she asked.

"Oh, they reserved judgment at first. But everyone who's had dealings with him seems to think he's 'a pretty good guy.' You know that's high praise around here. If he prefers not to bandy his personal affairs around, I guess they've decided that's his business. TJ says Cole Wyatt is about as decent and honorable a man as he's ever met."

TJ had been foreman here at the Circle C for a long time, and Jamie respected his opinion, just as her father had. She'd been a little dismayed to learn, on her return to McClintock, that the neighboring ranch had been sold to a complete stranger. She was relieved to learn that he was in good favor with the other ranchers in the area.

But did the man have to be so attractive?

Since he was her nearest neighbor, she wouldn't be able to avoid coming into contact with him now and then. She'd have to be on her guard around him, she thought, recalling that scene she'd witnessed in the library a few weeks ago. She didn't want to turn into a dithering idiot like poor little Miss Dowling every time he was in the vicinity.

Val's voice cut into her thoughts. "You know," she said, "you and Cole would be perfect for each other."

Jamie gave her friend a stern look. "The last thing I need is a man cluttering up my life. Especially after..." Her words trailed off.

"Don't let one bad experience ruin your life," Val advised. "All men aren't like Randy."

Jamie decided the conversation was becoming entirely too personal. "Why don't you go out in the kitchen and pour yourself a cup of coffee while I get dressed," she said, turning and heading for her bedroom.

Chapter Six

The door of the Back Forty swung open, as two patrons exited and set off down the street toward the next drinking spot. A burst of raucous laughter, mingled with the twang of country-western music, followed them.

Jamie shrank back into the shadows against the building, waiting for them to pass. She couldn't make herself as invisible as she'd hoped to, however, and one of the men slowed down, swaying slightly, to give her a speculative once-over. She returned his look with an icy glare, calculated to intimidate even the most determined. It evidently had the desired effect. After a moment of hesitation, he shrugged and threw an arm over his companion's shoulder, and the two merrymakers continued on their way.

Jamie watched their somewhat weaving progress until they turned the corner, then she headed toward the entrance to the Back Forty. As she pushed the door open, the combined odors of beer, too many bodies crowded into too small a space, and stale cigarette smoke almost caused her to change her mind. She'd come this far, though, she reminded herself. She might as well see it through.

When she'd made the decision to stay in McClintock and take over the Circle C, she'd had no illusions about what she was taking on. She'd been a rancher's daughter long enough to know running a cattle ranch was no tea party. She had forgotten, though, that her duties would include hunting down Emmett Stiles and making sure he got home safely.

Emmett had worked at the Circle C for as long as Jamie could remember and, aside from TJ, was the most valued employee at the place. Besides being intensely loyal, he could do the work of two men, and his knowledge of ranching was invaluable. In fact, he was almost the perfect ranch hand—except for one minor fault.

While most of the employees confined their more riotous behavior to Saturday night trips into town, Emmett shunned these weekly diversions, preferring to spend his off-duty time puttering around the ranch. Then every few months this strict adherence to the straight and narrow apparently got to be too much for him, and he threw caution and common sense to the wind and went on a monumental drinking spree.

When this happened, Jamie's father hadn't wasted time and energy getting upset over Emmett's behavior. He simply drove into town and made the rounds of the local bars until he located his errant employee, coaxed him out to the truck, and took him back to the ranch. Then he gently helped him into his bunk, and left him to sleep off the effects of his latest fall from grace. After a day or so, looking little the worse for wear, Emmett would be back on the job.

The ritual had been going on for as long as Jamie could remember. In between drinking bouts, Emmett was as faithful and hard-working an employee as anyone could hope for, and everyone—including Trace Cantrell—had learned to take his occasional lapses in stride. Although Trace wasn't a drinking man, he was tolerant of other people's weaknesses.

When it had come to Jamie's attention, a short while ago, that Emmett had gotten a ride into town with one of the other hands early this afternoon, and hadn't returned, she was well enough acquainted with his habits to figure out he was on one of his binges. He hadn't gone on one since she'd been back, so she supposed he was about due.

There was no getting around it; she'd have to go into town and look for him, and the longer she put it off the more difficult the task would be. Emmett would never make it home on his own. If left to himself, he'd simply continue drinking until he was in such a stupor that he could hardly put one foot in front of the other. She didn't relish prowling through McClintock's bars in search of a drunken cowhand, but it was one of those chores that, no matter how distasteful, just had to be done.

She vetoed the idea of sending any of her employees into town for Emmett. The only one she would have considered asking was TJ. In fact, TJ would probably have *insisted* on going after Emmett himself. But he had taken some much-deserved time off to accompany Val and their boys to Prineville to visit relatives, and wouldn't be back for several days.

Besides, she was aware that the entire crew had been watching her every move since she'd returned to take over the running of the Circle C, and that many of them had reservations about her ability to handle various situations that might come up. If she expected to have any credibility as ''the boss,'' she couldn't shift the unpleasant duties off onto someone else.

Drawing a deep breath, she pushed open the door of the Back Forty and entered.

Once inside, her senses rebelled against the blue haze of cigarette smoke that hung in the air, the stale beery smell, and the nasal twang of a country-western singer that blared from the neon-lighted jukebox.

As her eyes adjusted to the gloom, she let her glance sweep the room. A quick check confirmed that Emmett wasn't at any of the tables scattered about the front section of the place, or shooting pool over in the far corner. And she knew, without bothering to look, that he wouldn't be on the postage stamp–sized dance floor, where several couples swayed in time to the music. When Emmett went out drinking, he wasn't in the mood for shooting pool or socializing, and women scared him half to death.

If he was here, he'd be at the bar. That meant she'd have to go on in and look for him. And then if he wasn't here, she'd have to go through this again somewhere else. Although the Back Forty was his favorite drinking spot, she knew he sometimes branched out to some of the other establishments. The last thing she wanted to do was spend her evening going from one bar full of good ole boys to another, looking for him.

She hadn't taken more than ten steps when she became aware of a sudden hush in the room. Conversation had come to a halt, and the pool players in the corner had suspended their game while they leaned on their pool cues and regarded her with curiosity. Even the jukebox fell silent as Willie Nelson finished warning mamas of the hazards of letting their babies grow up to be cowboys. She had the feeling the entire room was holding its collective breath.

She should have realized she couldn't do this without drawing attention to herself. In spite of advances in gender equality in recent years, that good old double standard still existed in McClintock. Any woman who valued her good name just didn't go into places like the Back Forty unescorted. And considering her own already damaged reputation, she was simply adding fuel to the flame.

She fought the urge to turn around and walk out. If she expected her employees, as well as the other ranchers, to take her seriously, she couldn't chicken out the first time the going got a little rough. Drawing a deep breath, she assumed what she hoped was an air of casual indifference.

As she continued her progress toward the bar, a burly figure swaggered up and planted itself squarely in front of her, blocking her way. "Lemme buy you a drink," the man said, in a rough, demanding voice.

Jamie recognized him as Dewey Tate, a drifter who had worked for several of the ranches in the area. If memory served, he had been fired from his last job for being a "troublemaker." Her glance traveled upward, taking in the antagonistic expression, the stubble of beard on his chin, and his bleary eyes, indicating he'd had too much to drink.

"No thank you," she murmured. She tried to shoulder past him, but he refused to move out of her way.

"You too good to drink with me?" he demanded.

A flash of irritation ran through her. She'd hoped to get this over with, with as little fuss and bother as possible, but now this big dumb galoot was ruining everything. "It— it's not that. I just came in to—to—" To her dismay, her voice failed her.

Dewey's thick lips twisted into a sneer. "You got no call to be looking down your nose at me. Seems to me you're kinda particular about who you drink with. 'Course, maybe what they say about you is true, that you're more interested in married men—like Randy Mayfield." His words were accompanied by an insinuating leer.

The other patrons had been watching the scene with unabashed interest. Now a little murmur ran through the room, mingled with a few bursts of shocked laughter.

Although waves of embarrassment were washing over Jamie, she was determined not to give Dewey—or any of those watching—the satisfaction of knowing the effect his words had on her. "Let me by," she demanded, with as much authority as she could muster.

Dewey put a beefy hand on her arm. "Let's go have that drink," he said, urging her toward the bar.

Jamie had no intention of drinking with this brute. "Let go of me," she ordered. She attempted to pull her arm away but he held it in a viselike grip.

He chuckled. "Won't do you no good to fight me."

At first she'd been merely annoyed, but that annoyance began to give way to a feeling of apprehension. She'd thought he was just putting on a big macho act for the benefit of those around him. Now she realized how determined he was. Oh, she knew he couldn't force her into anything she didn't want to do, with all these people around. Still, she couldn't twist out of his grasp without causing a scene.

All at once she felt an arm come around her shoulders casually, and a familiar, husky voice was saying in her ear, "It's about time you got here, hon. I've been waiting for you."

The words seemed to come out of nowhere. Her eyes widened in astonishment as she glanced up to see Cole Wyatt at her side. She had no idea how he'd managed to approach without being noticed, but there he was.

He was the last person she was expecting to encounter here. Somehow, she hadn't pictured him as someone who would enjoy spending his time in a noisy, smoke-filled bar.

While she was still puzzling over this, he said, "You're late. I was wondering if you were going to make it."

Jamie opened her mouth to speak, but nothing came out. Her bewilderment increased as Cole leaned down so that his mouth was close to the sensitive spot just below her ear.

"Just play along," he whispered.

To anyone watching, it would appear that he was greeting her with a kiss. Even though his lips didn't make contact, she could feel his warm breath on her skin. In spite of the confusing jumble of thoughts running through her mind, she couldn't suppress the sudden, unexpected warmth that surged through her.

Straightening, he increased the pressure of his arm around her shoulders, and started to draw her away from Dewey. "Come on," he said. "There are a couple of empty stools at the bar."

"I—I'm sorry I'm late," she got out shakily. The welcoming smile she flashed him was genuine, as she tried to pull her arm away from Dewey.

Dewey didn't release his hold, though. Clearly, he was going on the old principle of possession being nine-tenths of the law.

"The lady's with me," Cole said pointedly to Dewey. "We have a date." His tone and manner indicated there was nothing more to be said about the matter.

Dewey's glance flicked from Jamie to Cole, and back to Jamie. He gave Cole a once-over. For a second or two he looked as if he might back down, but then he seemed to think better of it. "Me'n the lady are just gonna have a drink," he said, with a show of bravado. "There ain't nothin' wrong with that, is there?"

"I said she's with me." Cole didn't raise his voice, but there was no mistaking the understated warning in his words.

Dewey glared at him belligerantly. Tension hung in the

air like a thick curtain as the two men sized one another up. Although Dewey clearly outweighed Cole by at least fifty pounds, Jamie somehow sensed there was hardly a person in the room who wouldn't have put his money on Cole.

"Aw, she ain't worth fightin' over," Dewey growled out of the corner of his mouth. With that, he removed his hand from Jamie's arm and gave her a little shove toward Cole. Several patrons quickly stepped out of his path as he strode toward the door, glaring at anyone foolhardy enough to get in his way.

At that moment, the jukebox began to play again. The haunting, plaintive notes of Patsy Cline's "I Fall to Pieces" floated through the air. As if that were the signal for everything to return to normal, conversation resumed, couples drifted back onto the dance floor, and the pool players went back to their game.

Cole watched Dewey's retreating back until he was out the door. When he turned back to Jamie, she saw that his features were set into grim lines. "What are you doing in here?" he asked. Although he spoke low enough that others couldn't hear, there was an accusing note in his voice.

His tone sent a flash of resentment through Jamie. He sounded as if she were somehow at fault. She suppressed her annoyance, reminding herself that he *had* helped her out of what could have become a very touchy situation.

"I just came in to look for Emmett Stiles," she explained. "He—ah—sometimes drinks a little too much, and—"

Cole's understanding nod indicated that he was fully aware of Emmett's problem. "He's over at the bar. I was just about to get him out of here."

Jamie felt a twinge of uneasiness. Had Emmett been causing trouble? But that was unlikely. While some people might have a tendency to become unruly after a few drinks, she knew that Emmett, when he was in his cups, had always been as submissive and docile as a lamb. Still, she'd been away a long time, and people did change. She hoped he hadn't been causing a problem.

"I'll take care of him," she murmured. She headed toward the bar with the air of someone who was facing an unpleasant duty and had no choice but to see it through.

"You might need some help," Cole said, falling into step beside her. "I'll give you a hand."

She shot him a quick glance. "You don't have to do that. He's my responsibility."

Cole put a hand on her arm—not roughly, the way Dewey had done, but with just enough pressure to detain her so he could make his point. "What if you have trouble getting him into your truck?"

This was one of the problems that had been on Jamie's mind while she was driving into town. Even though Emmett was a wiry, slightly built little man, if he should happen to stumble and fall before she got him into the pickup, she wasn't sure she'd be able to help him up.

"Like I said, I'll give you a hand," Cole said, as if reading her mind. With his hand still on her arm, he steered her toward the bar.

They found Emmett staring morosely into an empty glass, as if reflecting on the imponderables of life. "C'mon, Emmett, time to go home," Jamie said softly.

Pulling his attention back from whatever private little world he'd retreated into, Emmett blinked several times, as if he were confused about exactly where he was. He offered no resistance when Cole and Jamie helped him to his feet and steered him toward the exit.

Jamie caught her breath sharply when he stumbled as she and Cole were maneuvering him out the door. He would have fallen if it hadn't been for Cole's firm, steady hand under his elbow.

With infinite patience, Cole helped him into the passenger seat of Jamie's pickup.

"Sorry to be such a bother," Emmett mumbled. "Don' mean to cause no trouble—"

"It's all right," Cole reassured him in soothing tones. Jamie couldn't help noticing there wasn't a trace of reproach or disapproval in his voice.

After making sure the seat belt was fastened securely around Emmett, Cole turned to Jamie. "I'd better follow you home."

"No, you don't need to do that," she protested. She had the uncomfortable feeling that she'd already allowed him to do too much for her. "I don't want to spoil your evening. Why don't you go on back inside?"

"Why would I want to do that?" He gave her a curious look, as if wondering where she'd gotten such an idea.

"I—I just thought—"

"I just came in to look for a rancher who has some stock for sale," Cole explained. "I found him, and made arrangements to go out to his place tomorrow and take a look at what he has, so there's no reason to stay here any longer. I was just leaving when I spotted Emmett. I figured I might as well take him home—save someone from the Circle C the trouble of coming in after him."

He glanced at Emmett, who was slumped down with his chin on his chest. "I'll follow you. You may need help getting him into his bunk."

He was right, Jamie realized. She might need assistance. This being Saturday night, there might not be anyone around to give her a hand with Emmett when she got him back to the ranch. His near fall a few moments ago had made her realize she couldn't handle him by herself. He wasn't a young man, and she had a sudden, disturbing mental picture of him lying on the ground with a broken hip or an even worse injury, because she'd been too stubborn or too full of pride to accept help when it was offered.

"Thank you," she murmured, getting into the truck and fitting the key into the ignition. "I appreciate it."

When she arrived at the ranch, she was glad she'd relented. Emmett had sunk into a semidozing state. It was obvious he wasn't going to be able to navigate under his own steam, and there didn't seem to be anyone on hand to help.

It was a relief when Cole pulled up behind her a few minutes later. With a quiet competence, he helped Emmett out of the truck and supported him as he guided him to the bunkhouse. Jamie hurried on ahead to open the door. After a quick glance inside to make sure the place was deserted, she went in to pull back the covers on Emmett's bunk.

She made a hasty retreat as Cole began to loosen Emmett's clothing. "Stop by the house when you're finished here," she said just before she slipped out the door. "I'll make some coffee."

Chapter Seven

Jamie realized her hands were shaking as she filled the percolator with water and measured out coffee. *Now what have I gotten myself into?* she wondered. For some reason, she found the prospect of being alone in the house with Cole late at night somewhat frightening.

She told herself to stop being ridiculous. He'd helped her out of a tough spot. The least she could do was offer him a cup of coffee. Besides, she couldn't avoid him forever. He *was* her closest neighbor. It might be a good idea to start letting herself become accustomed to being around him, to sort of work up an "immunity" to whatever it was that made her feel all weak and helpless whenever he was near.

The only sounds in the bunkhouse were Emmett's rhythmic snores as Cole removed the bandanna from around the older man's neck and unfastened his shirt. He slipped Emmett's boots off and, as an afterthought, unbuckled his belt.

After pulling the blankets up over the sleeping man, he aligned the boots next to the bunk with mathematical precision, then smoothed out the bandanna and carefully folded it into a square.

Catching himself, he wadded the piece of cloth into a ball and tossed it to one side. "What am I doing!" he muttered. He knew the reason for this sudden attention to neatness. He was putting off going up to the house.

It's just a cup of coffee, he reminded himself. Jamie had said she'd make coffee, and he supposed it would look— well, strange if he didn't stop in for at least a few minutes. Not that he'd ever been concerned about appearances, but since she was going to be living on the neighboring ranch, he supposed he'd have to make some effort to be on reasonably good terms with her.

It wasn't going to be easy. He'd spent most of his adult life avoiding becoming emotionally involved with anyone, quietly going about his own business, keeping to himself as much as possible and hoping others he came into contact with would do the same.

But that was B.J.—before Jamie. Now he found that she was invading his thoughts regularly.

It was more than a physical attraction—although he couldn't deny that that was certainly a factor. Every so often the memory of how warm and soft she'd felt in his arms would sneak up and take him by surprise. There was something else about her, though—maybe it was that *vulnerability* he'd sensed the first time he saw her—that brought out a streak of fierce protectiveness he hadn't known he possessed.

His thoughts went back to earlier this evening, in the Back Forty, when he'd been in the process of coaxing Emmett to come with him. He'd become aware of a certain tension in the atmosphere. Glancing around, he'd spotted

Jamie making her way through the crowded room, looking nervous and a little frightened, and trying to put up a brave front.

What is she doing here anyway, he'd wondered. Didn't she know how wild some of the local taverns could get on a Saturday night?

When Dewey Tate began to harrass her, he'd wanted to rush to her defense, especially after the big lout made that remark about "married men." He'd noticed the way she'd paled at that. He'd forced himself to keep out of the matter, though, reminding himself it was none of his business. It wasn't until Tate had had the audacity to put a hand on her that he decided it was time to step in. Although he'd tried to keep from making a scene, it had taken every iota of his self-control to keep from smashing his fist into the man's face. The recollection of that big rough hand on Jamie's smooth, silken skin still sent a rush of anger through him.

Jamie tried to suppress the little ripple of excitement she felt when she heard Cole's light tap at the back door. *Stop it,* she scolded herself. He was just coming in for coffee, for Pete's sake. After he gave her a report on Emmett, they'd make casual conversation for a few minutes, and when he finished his coffee he'd bid her a polite good-bye and be on his way. No big deal.

She arranged her features into an expression of impersonal courtesy as she opened the door. "Come in," she invited, stepping aside to allow him to enter.

Once he was inside, she began to wonder if this was such a good idea. She had underestimated that indefinable "something" that emanated from him—that aura of masculinity that both fascinated and frightened her.

All at once the normally adequate-sized kitchen seemed much smaller—hardly big enough for the two of them to move around in without bumping into each other. And it didn't help any that she hadn't turned on the overhead light, so the only illumination came from the small bulb over the counter. There was something so—so *intimate* about being alone in a dimly lit room with a man late at night.

She realized they were standing so close she could feel the heat from his body. She was shocked at the effect his nearness had on her.

With what little presence of mind she still had left, she took a step backwards, so suddenly that she almost lost her balance. Automatically, Cole put his hands on her shoulders to steady her. Even through her shirt, his touch made her skin tingle.

"I—I'll get you some coffee," she murmured, twisting out of his grasp and turning toward the counter. Making an effort to compose herself, she filled two mugs with the steaming coffee. As she handed one to him, she hoped he wouldn't notice the way her hands were trembling.

Their fingers brushed when he reached out to take the mug from her, and the light contact sent a jolt of electricity all the way up her arm. She jerked her hand back as if she'd touched something hot.

Had he felt it too? Jamie avoided meeting his eyes, afraid she'd give away too much of what she was feeling. Her gaze fastened on his hands as they closed around the mug. They were large, capable-looking hands, with strong, blunt fingers. She found herself wondering how those hands would feel on her skin, touching, caressing—

Good heavens, she thought, she had to get herself under control. "Milk? Sugar?" she managed to get out, gesturing toward the cream pitcher and sugar bowl on the counter.

"Black is fine," he said.

That seemed to exhaust the conversational possibilities for the time being. The silence lengthened, with the ticking of the kitchen clock the only sound in the room, as Jamie cast about for something to talk about. For the life of her, she couldn't think of a thing to say that didn't sound utterly inane.

She allowed herself a glance at Cole's face, but his expression, in the half light, was unreadable. As he took a sip of his coffee, he shifted his weight from one foot to the other. *Why, he's as nervous as I am,* she thought. Somehow, that knowledge didn't make her feel any more relaxed.

She began to wonder what in the world had possessed her to ask him to stop in in the first place. They had absolutely nothing in common. They'd never even had a real conversation.

Why *had* she invited him in?

Oh, yes—Emmett. "Did you get Emmett all squared away?" she asked, grabbing onto the subject of her ranch hand as if it were a lifeline.

Cole nodded. "He's sleeping like a baby." He seemed as relieved as Jamie to have come across a topic of mutual interest. "I unbuttoned his shirt and took off his boots, so he'd be more comfortable."

"That was thoughtful, but, considering the state he was in when we got him home, I doubt if he'd notice if he were sleeping on a bed of rocks."

"He'll probably wake up with the granddaddy of all headaches," Cole said, with what could almost pass for a smile. "Other than that, he'll likely recover with no ill effects."

"I appreciate your help tonight. I'm not sure I could have gotten Emmett out of the Back Forty and home by myself." Although she'd rather not discuss the Dewey Tate incident, Jamie hoped Cole understood that her blanket "thank you" included his intervention in that situation, as well as his assistance with Emmett.

Cole frowned, as if mention of the Back Forty brought to mind the events that had taken place there. The grooves that ran down either side of his mouth deepened, and the dim light of the kitchen cast stern shadows across his face, making him look even grimmer than usual. What had she said to elicit this kind of reaction, Jamie wondered. Was he angry because he'd been put in a position where he'd had no choice but to come to her aid?

"You shouldn't have been in the Back Forty," he said, his tone faintly accusing. "That's no kind of place for you to be going alone."

Jamie stared at him with a mixture of resentment and astonishment. What right did he have to lecture her?

She drew herself up to her full height, intending to make it clear to him that she was quite capable of taking care of herself. The words died on her lips, though, when it occurred to her that he was probably right. She *hadn't* been able to handle Dewey by herself. Although the knowledge was somewhat ego-deflating, she had to admit she might have been in real trouble if Cole hadn't stepped in when he did. Nobody else in the place had seemed inclined to come to her aid. Still, she felt he was being a little unfair. It wasn't as if she'd had a choice in the matter.

"*Somebody* had to go and look for Emmett," she pointed out.

"That should have been TJ's job," Cole snapped. "What was he thinking of, letting you go by there yourself?"

"I don't take orders from TJ," Jamie informed him coldly. "In case you've forgotten, *he* works for *me*, not the other way around."

"Then you should have 'ordered' him to go after Emmett." Cole's expression was stern and inflexible.

"TJ's out of town."

"Why didn't you send one of the other hands?"

Jamie could feel her anger rising. Who did he think he was, passing out advice as if she weren't capable of making her own decisions? "This is Saturday night," she reminded him. "Most of the hands have the night off. Besides, running a ranch is a tough business, as I'm sure you're aware. If I expect to gain the respect of the men who work for me, I have to let them know I'm not too delicate to take on the unpleasant tasks."

"There are some things a woman just shouldn't be doing," he maintained stubbornly. "If there really wasn't anyone around, you could have called me."

Her mouth dropped open in surprise. He couldn't be serious. "I wouldn't have dreamed of imposing on you that way," she said with dignity.

"No, you'd rather risk putting yourself in danger than ask for help," he shot back.

They stood toe to toe, glaring at one another. At first Jamie had thought he was simply reflecting the prevailing opinion of many of the males in the area, that all women were helpless little creatures who needed a man to protect them. But that wasn't in keeping with the things she'd heard about him. He'd practically made a career out of minding his own business, and letting others do the same. She felt her anger dissipating, replaced by a feeling she couldn't quite identify. In spite of her protests, an unexpected warmth spread through her at the knowledge that it actually mattered to him what happened to her.

"I—I wouldn't want to bother you with my problems," she said, regretting her defiant attitude. "Emmett isn't your responsibility."

The lines in Cole's face softened a little. "The next time you need something done that you can't handle alone, don't be afraid to ask for help," he muttered.

Jamie blinked back the sudden tears that stung her eyelids. She'd steeled herself to cope with doubts about her ability to run a ranch, as well as innuendos about her reputation. But his apparent concern about her safety and well-being, along with his offer of help, caught her with her defenses down.

Noting the change in her attitude, Cole felt a pang of self-reproach. He hadn't meant to upset her. Hadn't she already been through enough tonight? He'd only intended to impress on her that she might have been in danger. Although he wasn't in the habit of apologizing for his actions, he cast about for a way to take back his harsh words.

"Jamie, I—"

But whatever he'd been about to say faded from his mind as he found himself gazing into a pair of eyes as soft as a mountain mist. Something flickered in their smoky depths, something that stirred feelings long buried in him. Mesmerized, he was powerless to move or look away, despite the alarm that sounded in the back of his mind. His thoughts were suddenly tangled in a whirl of conflicting emotions. How could a man be expected to think clearly with those eyes holding his?

With a real effort of will, he pulled his gaze away, only to have it alight on her lips—soft, pink . . .

Although some vestiges of rationality cautioned him that he was teetering on the brink of what could only lead to disaster, he brushed the warning aside, aware only of the hunger inside him. The longing to hold her, to caress her silken skin and taste the sweetness of her lips overrode his usual Spartan self-control.

He reached out and drew her into his arms—not roughly, but with a gentle sureness.

She came to him willingly, with no hesitation. He could hardly believe how good it felt to hold her. He brushed his lips against hers, tentatively at first, tasting, sampling, then with more confidence, as he felt her mouth soften under his.

Jamie's heart lurched erratically and an incredible sweetness flooded her as she returned Cole's kiss. Her world spun dizzily . . .

She was jerked sharply back to reality by the sound of a vehicle pulling into the driveway. That would be some of the hands, returning from whatever Saturday night diversion they'd gone to. Her languid, unreal feeling vanished, as sanity returned.

Had she lost her mind? A few minutes ago she and Cole had been in the middle of a heated discussion. Then—somehow—she was in his arms, his lips were on hers.

A flush heated her skin. With a quick motion, she twisted out of his embrace.

Cole offered no resistance. Blinking in surprise, as if coming out of a trance, he dropped his arms and backed away. He seemed as taken aback as she over the unexpected turn of events. "I—I'm sorry," he apologized. "I don't know what got into me."

Jamie drew the bits and pieces of her shattered poise around her like a protective garment. "It was my fault as much as yours. There's blame enough to go around."

"Believe me, I never intended—"

Jamie felt a flash of irritation. Did he have to protest so much? "Forget it!" she snapped. "Sometimes things just—happen."

Judging by Cole's look of relief, he was only too glad to take her advice. Before Jamie's eyes, the lines of his face settled back into their usual mask of cool reserve. It was as if he'd suddenly realized how close he'd come to letting someone past the barrier he'd erected between himself and the rest of the world. She could almost see that barrier being reinforced, brick by brick.

He turned and made a hasty exit, a brief " 'Night,'' flung over his shoulder. Catching the door before it swung shut, Jamie peered after him until he disappeared into the darkness. A few seconds later she heard the roar of his truck engine, and saw the headlights cut into the darkness.

Instinctively, she touched her fingers to her lips, which still tingled from his kiss.

Cole drove the distance between the Circle C and the Lucky Horseshoe as if he were being pursued by wild animals. *That was a close call,* he thought. He had no idea what had gotten into him.

All he'd meant to do was make Jamie understand that, as her nearest neighbor, he was willing to lend a hand now and then if the need arose. Somehow, though, the image of Dewey Tate's hand on her arm, and the anger the sight had evoked in him, had gotten in the way of his common sense. The next thing he knew, he was caught up in the spell of those misty green eyes, of that soft, inviting mouth—

Resolutely, he put the memory out of his mind. Nothing like this must ever happen again, he told himself. Not that he hadn't thoroughly enjoyed kissing her. That was the problem. Without meaning to be, she was a threat to his zealously guarded sense of unapproachability.

Chapter Eight

The slight breeze coming in the door of the small kitchen of the McClintock Community Center did little except stir up the overheated air and move it around. Jamie brushed a limp strand of hair out of her eyes with the back of her hand.

It's your own fault, she reminded herself. *You don't have to be in here sweltering over a hot grill.* She could be outside, where the air was probably twenty degrees cooler. It had been her choice.

Her thoughts went back to when Warren Eagleton's wife Marianne had called her last week to say, "I know you said you were were going to be too busy at the ranch to take part in any of the Oregon Trail Days festivities, but— well, I need your help desperately. I'm on the planning committee, you know, and two of the people I had lined up to help with the pancake breakfast had to bow out. Unless I find replacements for them, the breakfast is going to

79

be a complete flop. If you come through for me, you'll have my undying gratitude.''

Jamie couldn't help wondering if the situation was really as dire as Marianne made it out to be, and not just a ploy to get her out among people. As Jamie's mother's oldest friend, Marianne sometimes seemed to feel it was not only her right, but also her duty to help pave the way for Jamie's reentry into the town's social life. She likely felt that an appeal to Jamie's sense of civic responsibility would be her best course of action. Just about everyone in town was expected to pitch in to make the annual weeklong celebration a success. Those who had no inclination to become involved in the planning and organizing were coaxed into donating goods or services.

''It'll give you a chance to see people you haven't seen in a long time,'' Marianne went on. ''Nearly everyone in town will be there, you know.''

Jamie did know. That was why she'd decided to stay away from the festivities. Her Uncle Frank and Aunt Nadine would likely be among those in attendance, and maybe Sheila and Randy. So far, she'd managed to avoid seeing her relatives since her return to McClintock, and they'd made no attempt to contact her. She supposed she'd have to get in touch with them sooner or later—Uncle Frank *was* her mother's only brother—but she wasn't looking forward to it. She knew that seeing them would only open up old wounds, and cause all the hurt to come flooding back.

It was difficult enough facing the other people of McClintock when she made her periodic trips into town to pick up supplies or take care of business matters. Oh, some of those she encountered welcomed her back warmly, but there were others who looked at her with obvious disapproval, as if wondering how she had the nerve to show her face around here again. And then there had been that incident in Roy Mayfield's hardware store . . .

Although she had the feeling she was being manipulated, she heard herself saying, "Well—if you really need me, I'll be glad to help." So here she was, mixing up seemingly endless batches of pancake batter, making sure the two big coffee urns didn't run dry, and that the supply of orange juice was replenished.

She was alone in the kitchen for the time being. When the rush had begun to taper off, the other volunteer workers had drifted outside to eat their own breakfasts and visit with friends before it was time to start cleaning up. The hum of conversation, interspersed with an occasional burst of laughter, reached her ears. Glancing out the window at all the people gathered in little groups around the picnic tables, lingering over coffee as they chatted with friends and neighbors, she felt a little pang.

There was nothing to stop her from joining them, she reminded herself. She could fix herself a plate, casually stroll outside, and find a spot to sit down and eat.

But she quickly abandoned the idea. If she walked up to one of the tables, would the people sitting there slide over to make room for her, or would she be completely ignored? Maybe it was cowardly of her, but she realized she wasn't ready to find out.

Turning away from the window, she was momentarily startled to see a man's figure silhouetted in the open doorway. He was carrying a large cardboard box. Although his features weren't discernible with the sunlight behind him, there was no mistaking Cole Wyatt's tall, lean form.

After that little scene in her kitchen the night he'd helped her with Emmett, she wasn't sure what her attitude toward him should be. She decided to take her cue from him.

As he stepped inside she noted, briefly, that there was a

bandage wrapped around his left hand. Although it had once been white, it was now somewhat soiled.

Now that he was no longer in silhouette, she was able to see his features. The grooves down either side of his face deepened into what was almost a scowl. He didn't seem at all pleased to see her.

"I brought some meat for the barbecue tomorrow afternoon." His tone was flat and impassive.

His cool manner sent a surge of irritation through Jamie. If he wanted to play it that way, she wouldn't dream of inflicting her company on him.

With a brief, impersonal nod, he went across the room to the small alcove, which held a restaurant-sized refrigerator. As he strode past her, she could see that the cardboard box in his arms contained a number of oddly shaped packages, wrapped in white butcher paper.

Cole muttered under his breath as he stowed his packages in the refrigerator. He'd forgotten that the pancake breakfast was this morning, until he'd driven up to the community center and seen all the vehicles in the parking lot and what seemed to be half the town milling around outside. His first impulse had been to turn around and leave, but he couldn't drive around in this hot weather with a side of beef in the bed of his truck.

Anyway, everyone seemed to be preoccupied with eating and socializing. If he was quick about it, he could slip inside, drop off the meat, and be on his way before anyone even noticed him. At least, that was the plan, until he'd found himself face to face with Jamie.

He supposed he *could* have shown a little more warmth, but he knew how risky even a small overture could be. He'd worked hard at keeping a wall between himself and others. So far he'd been fairly successful—at least until Jamie came along. Every encounter with her chipped away a little more of that wall, leaving him feeling exposed and vulnerable. His only defense was to stay away from her.

The trouble was, it seemed that fate, or happenstance, or whatever, was determined to thwart his plans. Even as simple a matter as making a delivery to the community center was as fraught with hazards as a minefield.

When he'd been asked to help with the Oregon Trail Days celebration, he'd said he would, only because he hadn't been able to come up with a good reason for declining.

It hadn't been as bad an ordeal as he'd expected. So far he hadn't been called on to do much except attend a meeting or two, where he'd managed to keep a low profile. His conscience had nagged him a bit because he wasn't "pulling his weight," but he'd eased his sense of guilt by offering to donate a side of beef for the upcoming barbecue. The offer had been readily accepted, enabling him to fulfill his obligation while still maintaining a certain distance between himself and the townsfolk.

At least, that was the way it worked in theory. If he'd had any warning that he'd be running into Jamie today, he could have prepared himself. But meeting her so unexpectedly, he'd been unable to stem the explosive currents that raced through him. As a defense mechanism, he'd covered his feelings with an attitude of indifference.

As he finished stowing the packages he'd brought in, he settled his features into an impersonal mask. He still had to make at least two more trips out to his truck for the rest of the meat.

He glanced into the kitchen warily. Jamie was at the counter and, although her back was toward him, it wasn't difficult to assess her mood. Everything about her—the stiff set of her shoulders, her quick angry movements—radiated annoyance. He strode quickly across the kitchen to the door.

Although Jamie was aware that Cole had gone out and come back in, she kept her back turned resolutely. What was wrong with the man, she wondered. Not that it mattered to her whether he ever gave her the time of day, she told herself. In fact, considering the effect he had on her, she'd be better off having no contact with him whatever.

Her thoughts were interrupted by a muffled groan—like a cry of pain—from the other room. It was followed immediately by a muttered exclamation.

She called out hesitantly, "Cole?"

No answer. "Cole," she repeated, "are you all right?"

After a few seconds he replied, "I'm fine."

He didn't sound fine, though. There was a sort of tightness in his voice. She wondered if she ought to peek in on him. After a few moments, her curiosity got the better of her. She went to the door of the alcove.

Cole was cradling his left hand in his right arm. His face, under his tan, was pale, and his mouth was set in a grim line. He had the look of a man in pain, although Jamie couldn't see any obvious signs of injury.

Then she noticed the dark red stain seeping through the bandage on his hand. His eyes met her challengingly. *Don't make a big deal out of this,* his expression told her.

All right, she thought, if he wanted her to pretend she didn't know he was injured and hurting, he could jolly well bleed to death. It would serve him right.

She reminded herself, though, that this was just typical male behavior. She recalled the time her father had been thrown from a horse and had stubbornly denied that he was hurt, despite a pronounced limp. When he'd finally gone to a doctor, at her mother's insistence, he'd been found to have a slight fracture. "If you'd waited much longer to come and see me, you could have done permanent damage to that ankle,'' the doctor had scolded. It occurred to her, with a little pang, that at least her father had had someone who cared enough about him to nag him into seeking treatment.

She weighed her options. She could either let Cole stand there and act as if nothing was wrong—and risk serious consequences—or take matters into her own hands.

She chose the latter.

Walking up to him, she held out her hand, in a way that indicated she didn't intend to put up with any beating around the bush about this. Cole's glance met hers, and for a second or two she thought he was going to give in without a fuss. Then his expression hardened, and he retreated behind his usual wall of reserve.

"It's nothing."

I can be just as tough as you, she told herself, refusing to be intimidated by his aloof manner. "Let me see that hand," she ordered, in her best schoolteacher voice.

Her no-nonsense approach had the desired effect. Cole blinked in surprise. Then, as if caught off guard by her authoritative manner, he slowly extended the injured limb.

Now we're making progress, Jamie thought as she carefully unwrapped the bandage. Her sense of satisfaction quickly turned to dismay, however.

The deep, jagged laceration that ran diagonally across the fleshy part of Cole's palm was red and angry-looking and the skin around it was taut and swollen. Although the cut had started to heal, one end of it had broken open—as if it had been reinjured—and blood was oozing out.

Jamie looked up at Cole, a question in her eyes. He lifted one shoulder in an indifferent shrug. "I was putting a new roof on the pump house, and I got in the way of a piece of jagged metal. It's just a scratch."

Jamie rolled her eyes heavenward. "First aid" had likely consisted of digging a handkerchief out of his back pocket and wrapping it around his hand while he finished his project. Then, later, he'd probably run some cold water over the wound and applied a hasty bandage. From the looks of it, it hadn't been changed since then.

"And then you reinjured it somehow today, and started it bleeding again." It was a statement, not a question.

Cole muttered something. His voice was so low Jamie couldn't make out his words.

"What was that?"

His mouth twisted into an expression of resignation. "I shut the refrigerator door on it," he admitted. His tone defied her to make any comment.

Jamie couldn't help wincing. That had to hurt like the dickens. She managed to keep her voice from betraying anything except a clinical interest, though. "This should have stitches, you know. Dr. Hadley's outside at one of the picnic tables. Why don't I go get him? His office is just down the street, and I'm sure he wouldn't mind—"

Cole's "No!" was sudden and explosive, as he tried to draw his hand away.

Jamie refused to relinquish her hold, though. "At least let me clean it up for you, and put a fresh bandage on it."

That closed look came over his face again. "I'll take care of it when I get back to the ranch."

A flash of anger ran through Jamie. Who did he think he think he was, anyway—Clint Eastwood? Like most of the men around here, he'd probably consider little, short of dismemberment, as sufficient reason for allowing anyone to "make a fuss" over him.

"I'm not proposing brain surgery!" she snapped. "All I want to do is wash off that cut and change the bandage.

Or do you intend to just tough it out until it gets infected and you end up having your hand amputated?''

She doubted if that was really likely, but her dire warning seemed to have the desired effect, judging by the look of alarm that came over his features. He covered it with a curt nod toward the injured limb. "I guess you could go ahead and put a bandage on it—or whatever."

He didn't need to act as if he were doing her a favor, she thought, but she managed to hold back the sarcastic response that sprung to her lips. "Come into the kitchen."

As she released his hand and walked over to the sink, she resisted the urge to glance over her shoulder to see if he was following. She had the feeling he might change his mind and bolt if she didn't tread very lightly.

She turned the taps on and adjusted the water temperature. "Now then—" she began. Turning around, she came up against Cole, who was standing directly behind her.

"Excuse me," she murmured, edging around him. "Stick your hand under the water and let it run a while," she ordered. As he did so, she got the first aid kit out of the cupboard and laid out the supplies she needed.

"There, that ought to be clean enough now." She turned the water off and held out a towel. "I don't suppose you remember when you last had a tetanus shot," she said as she patted his hand dry and inspected the wound.

There was that shrug again. "I'm not sure I've ever had one."

She considered suggesting he drop in to see Doc Hadley in the next day or so, to have that taken care of, but she doubted he'd heed her advice. Given his reluctance to allow anyone to "make a fuss" over him, he might just decide to forget the whole thing if she pushed the issue.

As she applied antiseptic ointment to the cut, pulled the edges together with a butterfly bandage, and wrapped clean gauze around his hand, she occasionally glanced up to see how he was doing. Although she was doing her best to be gentle, she realized how painful it must be to have her poking about an open wound. Yet he didn't indicate, by the slightest intake of breath or drawing together of his brows, that he was feeling a bit of discomfort.

He didn't have to be so stoic, Jamie thought. This tough guy attitude was beginning to irritate her. "Do you want a bullet to bite on?" she couldn't resist asking.

"What?" His puzzled frown changed to an expression of sheepishness as he recognized the touch of irony in her tone. "No thanks," he replied. "I'll just grit my teeth."

Jamie shot a glance at him. Was that an attempt at humor?

As Cole watched her small, capable hands tending the cut on his hand, something long dormant stirred inside him. It crossed his mind that he couldn't recall anyone ever being genuinely concerned for his well-being.before. He was experiencing a sensation completely foreign to him—a sort of vague warmth, that had nothing to do with either his injury or the attraction he felt for Jamie.

He must be getting soft, he thought, his mouth twisting into a wry grin. He told himself not to read too much into a simple act of kindness. She'd do the same thing for a stray dog that showed up at her door with an injured paw.

"There, that ought to do it," she said as she applied a final strip of tape to hold the gauze bandage in place.

Cole turned his hand one way and then the other, inspecting her handiwork. "Looks pretty good." He flexed the hand gingerly. "Feels better, too."

After that, there seemed to be little left to say. Still, for some inexplicable reason, Cole found himself reluctant to leave.

"How about some breakfast?" Jamie suggested.

The casual invitation caught him off guard. When he hesitated, she continued, "I'm sure nobody else is coming, and there's a lot of food left over. If somebody doesn't eat it, it'll just go to waste. You can eat in here." Her glance indicated the table in one corner of the kitchen.

"I—ah—wouldn't want to trouble you."

"It's no trouble at all," she assured him. "I can't start cleaning up until everyone else is done eating, so I might as well have something to do while I'm waiting."

Although community breakfasts were the kind of thing that ordinarily would have sent Cole running in the opposite direction, he found to his surprise that the inclination to "escape" wasn't as strong as it usually would have been under such circumstances. Maybe it was because his hand had finally stopped throbbing. For the first time since he'd injured it, he was relatively pain-free.

He realized Jamie was waiting for a reply. If he didn't say something soon, she was going to take his silence for acceptance. He couldn't seem to make himself voice the polite refusal that was on the tip of his tongue, though. The aromas of earlier cooking still lingered, reminding him that it had been hours since he'd eaten. And, as Jamie had said, he could remain in the kitchen. He could stick around long enough to have a bite to eat without compromising his privacy.

Chapter Nine

The burst of laughter that drifted in through the open window reminded Cole that half the town was just outside the community center. There was no telling who might come wandering in any minute.

His manner changed abruptly as he realized how close he had come to letting down his guard. "Thanks for the offer," he said, adopting a curt, businesslike demeanor, "but I—I still have the rest of the meat to put away, and I need to make some other stops before I head back to the ranch."

He thought he detected a brief glimpse of hurt in Jamie's eyes. He couldn't be sure, though, for it was replaced quickly by a cool mask of unconcern. "Of course," she murmured, turning away and busying herself at the sink.

Cole shifted awkwardly from one foot to the other. Admittedly, social skills weren't his strong point. Still, he supposed he didn't have to be quite so blunt in turning down the invitation. He tried to think of something he could say to soften the refusal, but nothing came to mind. Finally, with a helpless shrug, he turned and went out to his truck for the rest of the packages.

When he returned, Jamie was busy at the sink, her back to him. He hurried past her, anxious to be done with his errand and get out of here. He wondered how he'd gotten himself into a sticky situation like this, anyway. All he'd set out to do was to make a quick run into town, drop off his contribution at the community center, and be on his way.

His thoughts were interrupted by a male voice.

"Jamie—heard you were here—had to come in and see for myself."

Even though it was early in the day, the man's words were slurred, as if he'd been drinking.

He heard Jamie's little gasp of surprise—or was it alarm?

" 'Bout time you decided to come back to McClintock. I've missed you."

There was some kind of subtle insinuation in the tone that sent a stab of uneasiness through Cole. The voice was vaguely familiar—someone he'd spoken to around town—but he couldn't quite place it.

"Go away."

Cole sensed a pleading note beneath the bravado in Jamie's tone.

"Why, darlin'? We've got a lot to talk about."

"We don't have a thing to say to each other," Jamie shot back. "Just leave me alone."

Cole muttered under his breath. The last thing he wanted to do was to stand here and listen to—to whatever was going on between Jamie and this guy. He was even less inclined, though, to announce his presence by walking through the kitchen. It appeared the only sensible thing to do would be to simply wait it out and hope the confrontation came to a quick end.

The slurred voice drifted out to him. "Don' be that way, darlin'. We had something pretty good going for us."

Cole had no doubt that if he could see the man's face, he'd see that he was leering. He was surprised at the rush of anger that surged through him.

"That was before I had my eyes opened to just how awful you really are. And stop calling me darling," Jamie snapped. "Go on back to your wife, Randy."

Randy Mayfield. That was the voice Cole had been trying to place. The onetime high school football star, who now walked with a limp. And the wife Jamie had referred to? That would be Jamie's cousin, Sheila.

"Now, Jamie," Randy was saying, placatingly, "that's no way to be. No reason why we can't take up where we left off. If we're careful, there are lots of ways we can meet without Sheila finding out."

Although Cole had a sick feeling in the pit of his stomach at what Randy was suggesting, he reminded himself it was none of his business.

"You're disgusting." There was no mistaking the contempt in Jamie's voice.

"Kinda uppity for someone with a reputation like yours, aren't you?"

Cole's jaw clenched tightly. He'd heard enough to know the man's attentions were unwelcome to Jamie. He fought down a sudden urge to confront this joker, to take him out behind the building and teach him a lesson. *Stay out of it,* he told himself. True, he'd gone to Jamie's aid that night she'd been accosted by Dewey Tate in the Back Forty, but that was different. Dewey had been trying to force her to go with him. Randy was only shooting his mouth off. Besides, he couldn't go around rushing to her defense every time she got into a sticky situation.

His lips twisted into a sardonic grin at the image of himself as a knight in shining armor, rescuing damsels in distress . . .

His thoughts were interrupted by Jamie's voice: "Just go away and leave me alone." The tired, pleading note—as if she had little strength left for fighting—went straight to his heart, awakening sensations he couldn't quite identify.

He had to get out of there, he told himself. He had the panicky feeling that if he didn't, he was going to find himself involved in something that was none of his concern. Although he'd almost rather face a grizzly bear than let these two people in the kitchen know he was listening in on their conversation, he couldn't stay here indefinitely, an unwilling eavesdropper. The only way he could extricate himself from this situation was to simply stride past them and out the door.

" 'Oughta be a little nicer to me," he heard Randy say in a wheedling tone that was like fingernails scraping down a blackboard. "Don' forget whose fault it is I've got this bad leg."

"You know as well as I do who caused that accident, and it wasn't me!" Jamie shot back, as if that last remark had triggered a renewed burst of fighting spirit in her. Cole could picture the high color in her cheeks, and the emerald-toned sparks shooting from her eyes.

"You think anyone's gonna believe you?" Randy taunted.

Cole edged closer to the connecting door and glanced into the kitchen. Randy was leaning back against the counter in an insolent slouch, and Jamie was facing him. Her purposeful stance left no doubt about her feelings. Anger radiated from every particle of her being.

Cole realized that if he ever intended to make his break, the time was now. He could only hope Jamie and Randy would be so involved in their heated discussion that they would pay little attention to him.

But before he could make his move, the screen door opened and, from his vantage point, he saw a tall, slender woman with a wealth of red hair join the two people in the kitchen. It crossed his mind, briefly, that she would have been pretty, if it hadn't been for the hostility that marred her features. Grumbling under his breath at this unforeseen complication, Cole ducked back out of sight.

"I might have known I'd find you in here—with *her*." The red-haired woman spat the words out contemptuously.

"Sheila, babe—this isn't what you think. Jus' came in to welcome Jamie back. Don' forget, she *is* family." It was obvious, from Randy's mocking manner, that it mattered little to him whether or not she believed him.

Arrogant pup, Cole thought, shifting his position slightly. The movement brought the trio back into his line of vision. He saw the resentful glare the red-headed woman—Sheila—shot toward Randy.

"I guess it's time for me to make myself scarce," Randy said, in a tone that made Cole long to put a fist into that handsome face. "I know you and your cousin have a lot to talk about." With that, he sauntered out the door.

Once he was gone, Sheila whirled to face Jamie. "I'm warning you, leave my husband alone!"

Jamie's chin went up a fraction of an inch. "I'm not interested in Randy. I wouldn't have him as a gift."

"Oh, come off it," Sheila said. "You know you can hardly stand it that he married me instead of you."

"I won't deny it was embarrassing to have the whole town know he'd thrown me over for you," Jamie replied. "After I thought about it, though, I realized a little embarrassment was a small price to pay for having found out just what he was really like. You probably did me the biggest favor of my life by taking him away from me.'' The only outward indication that her cousin's taunts had hit their mark was the sudden flush that stained her cheeks.

''Surely you don't expect anyone to believe that, when you were with him the night of the accident.'' Sheila's tone was contemptuous.

''They *would* believe it,'' Jamie said, slowly and evenly, ''if you'd told the truth about what I was doing with Randy.''

''Why should I? Only you and I know what really happened that night, and *I'm* certainly not going to tell anyone. It's more fun having people think my sweet, innocent little cousin was carrying on with my husband.''

''You're really going to go on letting everyone believe there was something between Randy and me?'' Jamie asked. She sounded incredulous.

''You'd better believe it,'' Sheila drawled. ''Everyone always thought you were so perfect. You can't imagine how much I enjoy seeing my rival's reputation in shreds. All my life I've had to hear about how terrific you were. 'Jamie is editor of the school paper' '' she mimicked sarcastically. '' 'Jamie is class valedictorian. Isn't that wonderful!' ''

Cole didn't miss the resignation in Jamie's sigh. ''Sheila, the only rivalry between us was in your own mind. You had your share of accomplishments. You were head cheer leader. You were homecoming queen. You had the lead role in the senior class play.''

''Only because you broke your ankle and had to be replaced. I should have had that part to begin with—but you always got everything I wanted. It's time the people of

McClintock found out you're not the paragon of virtue they always thought—''

Sheila's scathing words were interrupted by the arrival of two more of the kitchen volunteers—Lloyd and Edwina Cramer, who ran a real estate office in town. "We didn't mean to leave you by yourself with all the work," Edwina apologized. "We were having such a good time out there, talking and visiting—" Her words trailed off as she saw that Jamie wasn't alone. She and her husband glanced from Jamie to Sheila curiously, as if they sensed a certain tension in the air.

"I just popped in to say hi to my cousin," Sheila said sweetly, rising to the occasion. "I wanted to make sure she knows I don't bear her any ill will, in spite of all that's happened. I believe in letting bygones be bygones."

As Sheila took her leave, Jamie stared after her, frustrated. When she'd arrived here this morning for her stint in the kitchen, it had been obvious that some of the other workers, including Lloyd and Edwina, weren't altogether comfortable about working with her. She couldn't blame them, after the lurid tales that had circulated about her. As the morning wore on, they'd begun to warm up to her, though, as if the possibility was starting to occur to them that some of those stories might not be altogether true.

Jamie had taken that as a good sign that the scandal might eventually blow over. Now she realized how unlikely that was, with Sheila around to fan the flames. With a few well-chosen words, her cousin had not only managed to reinforce the idea of Jamie's guilt, but to establish her own image as the wronged but forgiving wife.

She felt as if a dull, heavy lump had settled in the pit of her stomach. Was that story going to follow her around for the rest of her life? She started to fill the sink with hot water, so she could start washing the dishes. The sooner the cleaning up was done, the sooner she could escape the prying eyes and curious looks.

She realized Edwina was scrutinizing her closely. "Are you all right, dear?" she asked, her tone solicitous. "You're as pale as a ghost."

"Oh—it—it's just that it's a little warm in here," Jamie stammered.

Edwina was immediately concerned, as well as apologetic. "We never should have allowed you to stay in here in all this heat," she said. "We should have insisted you come outside where it was cooler, and have breakfast with us. Why don't you run on home, dear, and let us finish up here. You've already done more than your share."

"Oh, I couldn't—"

"Of course you could. You've been in here working all morning, and anyone can tell you're completely worn out. You need to go home and lie down."

Although Jamie would have liked nothing better than to follow Edwina's suggestion, she felt duty-bound to fulfill her commitment. "At least let me help clear the tables."

"Absolutely not," Edwina replied firmly. "Lloyd and I will do that. Now then, do you need someone to drive you?"

When Jamie assured them she could manage on her own, they gave her a few last-minute instructions, such as, "Go straight home and rest," and, "Be sure to drink lots of liquids," before hurrying off to clear the tables.

Jamie had every intention of following their advice, but she needed a moment or two to pull herself together before she went outside. The confrontations with her ex-fiancé and her cousin had taken more out of her than she cared to admit. In spite of her assurance to Edwina and Lloyd that she was fine, she felt utterly shaken. In her present state of mind, she was afraid that anything—even a kind word—might cause her to burst into tears.

No, I will not cry, she told herself. She was going to be running into Sheila and Randy often now that she was back, so she might as well get used to it. It was just that—well, until now she'd been able to at least pretend the stories circulating about her and Randy had been the result of misinformation. Now she could no longer pretend. By Sheila's own admission, she'd deliberately set out to tear Jamie's reputation to shreds. That knowledge, coupled with Randy's unwelcome attentions, made her wonder if her decision to come back had been wise. Maybe she'd have been better off, after all, selling the ranch and going someplace else, where she could make a new life for herself.

But the Circle C was her home. She had every right to be here. In spite of her determination to not cry, tears stung her eyes at the unfairness of her situation.

Edging over to the door and peering into the kitchen, Cole saw with relief that Jamie was once again alone. If he was going to get out of here without too much embarrassment to either himself or Jamie, he'd better get moving now. He didn't especially care to have her know he'd overheard remarks not intended for his ears, but he reminded himself he'd had little choice. He hadn't asked to be trapped in this little room, forced to listen in on personal matters. He didn't intend to hang around long enough for it to happen again, though. There was no telling who else might come sauntering in if he didn't get going.

Steeling himself, he stepped into the kitchen. His original intention was to simply stride past Jamie and out the door. If they happened to make eye contact, he'd nod briefly and keep on going.

Without meaning to, he slowed to a halt, though, at the sight of the small figure standing by the sink. She looked fragile and defenseless and—the word that had come to mind the first time he'd seen her popped into his head now—vulnerable.

Something twisted deep inside him, as some hitherto buried emotion surfaced. He couldn't put a name to it—pity, sympathy, protectiveness? He only knew, on some basic level that had nothing to do with rational thought, that he couldn't just walk off and leave her this way.

In a few strides, he was standing in front of her. Slowly, Jamie raised her head. He saw that her eyes were misty, as if she were holding back tears.

"Y-you've been here all this time? You heard—"

He nodded.

"I'm sorry you had to get caught in the middle of that," she apologized. She summoned a weak smile, and he could tell she was making a valiant attempt to downplay the scene he had just been witness to. "You know how these family spats are—" Her slender hold on her self-control deserted her, and her voice broke in a sob.

Cole considered himself equal to just about any situation, but now he was at a complete loss. It was the first time he'd ever found himself in the position of having to offer comfort to another person. Finally, acting on pure instinct, he put his arms around her, somewhat hesitantly.

She offered no objections as he drew her close. Lord, he thought, she wasn't much bigger than a kitten. When she rested her head against his chest, the trusting gesture melted the last of his resistance. That simple movement of hers released a flood of unfamiliar sensations. This fragile little person in his arms actually *needed* him, needed whatever strength and support he could offer. That knowledge aroused such a fierce protectiveness in him that he was surprised at the force of of his emotions.

At that moment, he would willingly have fought off

mountain lions, or stood between her and a raging forest fire. There was little he could do, however, to protect her from the unwelcome attentions of an ex-fiancé or the malicious taunts of a jealous relative.

Keeping one arm around her, he fumbled in his back pocket for a handkerchief. He held it out to her and she accepted it wordlessly. As she daubed at her eyes in a vain attempt to stem the flow of tears, he patted her shoulder awkwardly.

When at last she seemed to be all cried out, she gave a little shuddering sigh, a soft helpless sound that went straight to his heart. Removing his arm from around her small frame, he put a work-roughened finger under her chin and tilted her face up to his. He took the handkerchief from her, intending to wipe away the last of the tears, but his hand hesitated as her shimmering green eyes caught and held his. A man could get lost in those eyes . . .

He was yanked sharply back to reality by the sound of approaching voices. Glancing over Jamie's head, he saw Lloyd and Edwina heading toward the building, bearing trays of dishes. Hastily, he dropped the arm that was around Jamie, stuffed the handkerchief back into her hand, and walked outside without a word.

As he neared the couple, they glanced at him curiously. Composing his features into an impersonal mask, he touched the brim of his hat. " 'Morning, folks," he said with a brief nod, as he strode past them.

Chapter Ten

Cole's brow furrowed as he concentrated all his energy into wielding the post hole digger, attacking the job as if his life depended on it.

Levi glanced into the hole Cole had just dug. "You planning to dig your way to China? Them holes don't need to be that deep."

"I—ah—guess I wasn't thinking," Cole said, nudging some of the dirt back into the hole with his boot.

" 'Pears to me you ain't been doing a whole lotta thinking lately," the old man observed. "Leastways, not about what you're doing."

Cole glanced at him sharply. "What's that supposed to mean?"

Levi's leathery face was the picture of innocence. "Nothing much. 'Cepting that yore mind seems to be somewhere else these days."

"Ranching's a serious business," Cole said testily. "It takes a lot of advance planning to keep things running smoothly. I was just thinking ahead, trying to decide when we ought to move the herd down to the south pasture, and whether those irrigation pipes need replacing yet.''

''You sure there ain't something else on your mind?'' Levi asked, as he and Cole maneuvered a new post into the hole he'd just dug and tamped the dirt around it.

''I don't know what you're talking about.'' Cole's tone made it clear the subject was not open to discussion.

Levi's comments had hit a little too close to home. He *had* been preoccupied lately—and it wasn't ranching that was claiming so much of his attention. Just when he was least expecting it, he'd find himself remembering that episode a few days ago when, acting on pure instinct, he'd reached out to Jamie to offer comfort and solace. He still wasn't sure what had caused him to do something so completely out of character. He only knew that the sight of her, in that attitude of vulnerability, had touched something in him, something he hadn't known existed.

He was already resigned to the fact that he wasn't immune to Jamie's physical attributes. He'd naively thought he could ignore the effect she had on him, though, until that time his emotions had gotten in the way of his better sense and he'd taken her in his arms and kissed her. That had alerted him to the reality that—where Jamie was concerned—he had about as much backbone as a jellyfish.

Once he was aware of the danger, he'd concentrated on steeling himself against that sudden longing he felt at every encounter with her. He thought he was doing fairly well. By exercising every iota of his will power, he could go for long periods of time—hours, perhaps—without allowing himself to think about how she fit so nicely into his arms, how warm and yielding her lips felt under his . . .

He jabbed the post hole digger into the ground as if he were fighting off the memories.

No, it wasn't the physical attraction that was a problem, he admitted. What scared the daylights out of him was finding out how easily she could penetrate that wall he'd erected around his emotions. He knew that once he started giving ground, it would be almost impossible to get it back.

Levi's gravelly voice broke into his thoughts. "Looks like we got comp'ny, Boss."

Cole looked up to see Jamie's pickup pulling into the driveway, as if thinking about her had conjured up her presence. Frowning, he glanced at the older man, a question in his eyes.

Levi shrugged, as if to say, *Beats me, Boss*. Both men watched—Levi with frank curiosity and Cole somewhat warily—as Jamie alighted from the truck, carrying a small white case of some kind. Cole found himself torn with mixed emotions. Although the part of his brain that dealt with common sense and rational thinking warned him to keep his distance, another part of his mind couldn't suppress a rush of sheer pleasure at the sight of her.

Jamie drew a deep breath. If she were to follow her instincts, she would get back into her truck and drive away as if her life depended on it. Everything in her shrank from facing Cole again after that morning, a few days ago, when she'd lost control and cried on his shoulder. Her cheeks burned at the memory.

She reminded herself that she was here on an errand of mercy. That injured hand of Cole's was likely to become seriously infected without some follow-up treatment. She'd tried telling herself it was none of her business, that he was a grown man and certainly capable of looking after himself. If he was too stubborn to take proper care of the injury, he'd just have to suffer the consequences.

Her conscience wouldn't let her dismiss the situation that easily, though. She'd never been able to bear seeing any living creature hurt or in pain. Even as a child she was always bringing home injured animals to clean and bandage their wounds—sometimes against their strenuous objections. Cole reminded her a little of some of those animals—in need of help but wary of allowing anyone to get too close. It appeared that she was going to have to take matters into her own hands. She hoped he wasn't going to misjudge what was strictly a humanitarian gesture. It was too late to back out now.

"I came over to take a look at your hand," she said, trying to sound matter-of-fact.

After a moment of silence, Cole replied, in clipped tones, "I appreciate your concern, but it doesn't need any more attention. It's coming along fine. It's almost healed." To demonstrate, he flexed his hand.

Jamie couldn't help noticing that he winced slightly as he did so. The fleeting expression of pain, although he covered it quickly, reinforced her resolve. She'd expected him to take this attitude, and she was prepared to stand her ground. Having already seen evidence of how unlikely he was to take care of the injury, she doubted he'd done anything, beyond replacing the bandage she'd applied several days ago.

"I don't have time to stand around and argue," she said. "It's going to get infected if it isn't taken care of." She'd found that, when dealing with her enigmatic neighbor, a businesslike, impersonal manner worked best. Anything else was likely to send him retreating back into his shell.

The two men glanced at one another, their eyes widening in surprise. Levi was the first to recover his equilibrium. "Sounds like she means business, Boss," he drawled. "If I was you, I'd do what she says." Although his tone was serious, there was a twinkle in his eye.

Turning his attention back to Jamie, Cole said, "Well, we're—ah—pretty busy right now—"

"You go ahead." Levi took the post hole digger from him. "I'll finish up here."

Cole glared at him, but Levi seemed cheerfully unaware of the hostile looks directed his way by his employer.

Various expressions played across Cole's features, from caution to grudging acceptance. "I guess you might at well change the bandage," he said finally. "As long as you're here anyway."

"Let's get on with it, then." Jamie started toward the ranch house, glancing over her shoulder to say, "Come on. The sooner it's done, the sooner you can get back to work."

With an air of resignation, Cole followed her to the house.

Jamie wasn't sure what to expect when he opened the back door and stepped aside so she could enter. She knew many of the men around here would only stoop to washing dishes or sweeping a floor when the situation became desperate.

She was pleasantly surprised as she stepped into the big ranch kitchen. The room was neat and well-organized. There were even a few homey touches, such as a colorful throw rug on the floor in front of the sink, and a big, comfortable-looking rocking chair by the window. She'd expected him to be as Spartan in his household arrangements as he was in other aspects of his life.

Cole submitted without too much protest as she removed the bandage from his hand. "It's looking pretty good—under the circumstances," she said, inspecting the wound.

That wary expression came over his features again. "Under *what* circumstances?"

"Well, operating a post hole digger didn't do it a lot of

good. Especially with the weather as dry as it's been around here lately. That ground is like concrete." She turned the tap on. "Stick your hand under there."

He did as she directed, but not without a scowl, a look he had perfected to discourage those who meddled too closely into his affairs. It didn't seem to have the desired effect on Jamie, though. "If there's work to be done, some-body has to do it," he pointed out.

"I can't believe you're the only one on the place who knows how to dig holes," she said, drying his hand. "Is that a specialized skill?" Her serious demeanor belied the touch of mockery in her voice.

Cole's brows drew together in a frown. "I'm the boss," he said defensively. "I can't shirk my duty just because I've got a little scratch on my hand."

"That's just it. You *are* the boss. You have a whole crew of men who get paid to follow your orders."

"I have to set a good example."

Opening the first aid kit she'd brought along, Jamie took out a tube of antiseptic ointment. "I seem to recall a while back you told me if something came up that I couldn't handle, I should ask for help. You were quite adamant about it, in fact."

"That was different—"

"The principle is the same," she replied, as she gently applied ointment to the wound. "You've really been very lucky, you know. It's a wonder this didn't become in-fected."

"I'm too tough to get infections," he replied wryly.

"Or too stubborn," Jamie murmured under her breath.

"What?"

"Nothing." She arranged her features into an impersonal mask as she wound a fresh bandage around his hand.

"There," she said when she was finished. "That ought

to—'' Her words were cut off by a sudden clap of thunder. Involuntarily, she emitted a little startled cry.

She let her breath out slowly as the last rumbling died away. ''That was too close for comfort.''

''I've had a feeling there was a storm in the air,'' Cole said. ''The animals have been acting up.''

''Well—ah—I'd better get going.'' Jamie couldn't quite keep her fingers from trembling as she began packing the first aid supplies back into their container. She felt a sense of urgency. Out here where sections of the road were unpaved, a heavy downpour could turn the dust into a slippery, semiliquid layer on which it was almost impossible to maintain any traction.

She'd had a fear of driving under those conditions ever since . . .

''If you were planning on beating the storm, looks like you're too late,'' Cole said, as the first heavy drops of rain began pelting the window.

An exclamation of dismay escaped Jamie as she glanced outside. Although rainstorms were rare in eastern Oregon during the summer, when they did occur they were usually sudden and violent. This one was already showing signs of becoming a real gully washer. Through the window, she could see Levi making a run for the shelter of the barn.

''If I get started right now, maybe I can beat the worst of it,'' she said, picking up the first aid kit and turning to leave.

At her utterance of alarm, Cole had raised an eyebrow questioningly. Now, in a movement so casual it seemed completely unplanned, he sauntered over to the door, reaching it a second or two before she did. Arms folded, he stood looking down at her, effectively blocking her way. ''You're not really planning to go out in that?''

Jamie wished he weren't standing quite so close, but she

didn't want to step back. It would seem as if she were . . . retreating. "If I don't leave right now, I'll be stranded here until the storm is over."

The lines in his face deepened. "It's not exactly a fate worse than death."

"I—I just meant—I don't want to take up any more of your time. I'm sure you're busy—"

"There's not much I can do until the rain lets up. I'm pretty much stuck in here myself."

"But I wouldn't want to impose on you."

"Look, you're not imposing!" he snapped. Then, as he regretted the brief outburst, his manner softened. "Is it so hard for you to swallow your pride and accept anything from anyone?"

Jamie's mouth dropped open in surprise. She was tempted to point out that he—Mr. Independence himself— was the one who almost had to be forced at gunpoint to allow his injured hand to be treated. She bit off the words, telling herself she was making too big a thing out of this. He was only doing what any well-meaning person would do, offering her the shelter of his home during a storm. She'd be foolish to insist on leaving, the way the rain was coming down.

She managed a smile. "I'm sorry," she said contritely. "Of course I'll be glad to stay until the storm is over."

Cole nodded, as if acknowledging his approval that she had come to her senses. He wasn't as calm as his outward demeanor would suggest, though. The storm was likely to last an hour or two. It wasn't going to be easy being close to her all that time, trying not to let her see that it was all he could do to keep from taking her in his arms . . .

A low rumble of thunder interrupted his thoughts, which was just as well, he told himself. That line of thinking could only lead to trouble. "Looks like we're in for a long wait.

Why don't we go into the living room, where we'll be more comfortable," he said briskly.

He filled two mugs with coffee from the pot on the stove, and handed one to Jamie. She murmured her thanks as he ushered her through the door.

Jamie glanced around the spacious room, which was furnished with a long, low sofa and several large, comfortably shabby chairs. In one corner was a television set, with a VCR on the shelf below it and videos stacked on top of and around it. A makeshift bookcase on the other side of the room was filled to overflowing. She had the feeling the room was a hideaway, a sanctuary for someone who preferred the company of books to that of other people.

She felt a brief stab of panic at the realization that she and Cole were going to be forced to spend the next hour or so in one another's company. What in the world would they find to talk about? Right now she couldn't think of a thing she had in common with this distant, unapproachable man. Hesitantly, she lowered herself into an easy chair, wrapping her arms around herself in an instinctively protective gesture.

"Cold?" Cole asked, misinterpreting the action. "I'll get a fire going." He touched a match to the pile of wood and kindling in the fireplace, and it sprang into flame.

Although the warm glow helped disperse some of Jamie's edginess, she still didn't feel entirely comfortable. As the silence in the room lengthened, she resisted the urge to drum her fingers on the table next to her chair. Taking a sip of coffee, she eyed Cole over the rim of her coffee mug. He appeared as ill at ease as she was.

This is ridiculous, she thought. They were reasonably intelligent adults. They ought to be able to come up with a topic of conversation. The only thing that came to mind, though, was, *Boy, it's really coming down out there.*

From where she sat, she could see the titles of some of the videos stacked on the VCR. "I see you like the same movies my dad did." Although the comment might not win any prizes for sparkling repartee, it beat sitting around listening to the rain come down.

Cole looked relieved to have something to talk about. "Yes, Trace and I often traded movies and books. We had a lot of the same tastes."

"You and my dad were friends, then?"

Cole nodded. "I was on pretty good terms with both of your parents." He took a sip of coffee. "You might have noticed—I'm not one for getting too close to people—"

Jamie resisted an urge to say, *Boy, you can say that again.*

"—but—well, your folks were fine people. I had a lot of respect for both of them. I never got around to telling you how sorry I was when they died. You must miss them a lot."

"Thank you," Jamie murmured. "I do miss them." She swallowed the lump in her throat. "I'm sorry now that I stayed away so long. We lost so much time that we could have had together. I guess, like most people, I had a tendency to think my parents would be around forever . . ."

"You had no way of knowing."

"Just the same, I should have been here. I wanted to come home so many times, but, well, every time I thought about what I'd have to contend with if I did come back, I guess I just didn't have the courage to face up to it." She toyed with the coffee mug in her hand. "You were in on that charming little scene that took place at the community center, so you have some idea. Between my cousin Sheila making sure the gossip about me never had a chance to die down, and her husband Randy—"

She made an effort to compose herself. "I'm sorry. I'm

sure the last things you want to hear about are my personal problems.''

Something twisted inside Cole as he noticed the way her voice broke—and how hard she tried to hide it. ''Want to talk about it?'' he heard himself asking. ''Sometimes it helps to get things out in the open.''

Once the words were out, he could hardly believe he'd said them. He'd always run like a scared rabbit from anything that remotely resembled emotional intimacy with another person. He kept personal matters to himself, and expected those around him to do the same. Now here he was encouraging Jamie to talk about things that should be of no concern to him. What was it about this woman that brought out a side of himself he'd carefully kept hidden for most of his life?

Carrying her coffee mug, Jamie got up and went to the window, where she stood watching the rain come down. She was silent for so long Cole began to wonder if he'd offended her. Did she feel he was prying into her private life? Why hadn't he just kept still?

Chapter Eleven

"I'm sure you must have heard the talk about Randy and me," Jamie said, after several moments of silence. "People in McClintock love to gossip."

"I—ah—did hear a few things," Cole acknowledged with a shrug. "I'm not one to pay much attention to what other folks say, though."

"I was engaged to him once, you know, when I was young, and not a very good judge of character." She gave a bitter little laugh. "I can't imagine what I ever saw in him, but I guess I was just sort of dazzled at first. He was good-looking, and had been a football star back in high school. By the time I realized what he was really like, I didn't know quite how to go about breaking up with him." She paused for a moment before going on. "Then he solved that problem for me when he and Sheila ran off and got married."

She said these last words in a flat, unemotional tone, simply stating a fact. Cole refrained from voicing his opinion—that the guy couldn't have been any bargain to begin with if he hadn't at least had the decency to break the engagement before marrying someone else. Or that he'd like to search out young Mayfield and wring his smart-alecky neck.

Kneeling down on one knee, he began stoking the fire-place with a poker. "Sounds to me like you were lucky to be rid of him," he said, not looking at her.

"It was as much Sheila's fault as Randy's, of course," she went on. "Not that I'm making excuses for him, but I'm quite sure Sheila wanted to make sure the whole town knew he'd thrown me over for her."

Unaccustomed to being put in the position of confidant, Cole could think of no response to this. Besides, he sensed she was talking more to herself than to him, as if this was something she'd kept hidden inside her for too long and needed to get out into the open. Instinct told him to keep quiet and let her talk. He placed another log on the fire and shoved it into place with the poker.

Jamie waited for a long, drawn-out growl of thunder to die away before she continued. "All our lives, Sheila wanted everything I had. I've never understood why—I certainly never wanted to be in competition with her. I think it was mostly her mother's fault. Aunt Nadine—she's married to my mother's brother—always pushed Sheila to outdo me." She didn't sound bitter, just resigned, as if this were something she'd learned to accept.

"I don't mean it was Aunt Nadine's idea for Sheila to take Randy from me. By the time we were grown, I guess the habit of wanting whatever I had was ingrained in Sheila. And I suppose Randy must have seemed like the ultimate prize."

Cole stopped poking around in the fireplace, and glanced over at Jamie. She was still standing at the window, her

back to him, watching the rain. She looked small and fragile—defenseless.

Putting the poker back in its holder, he dusted off his
hands and got to his feet. After a moment of hesitation, he
came over and stood behind her. ''I'd say the two of them
deserve each other,'' he commented.

''Everyone thought I was being 'terribly brave' because
I didn't seem to be too broken up. The truth was, I was
just relieved. I tried to avoid both of them, but that wasn't
easy in a town the size of McClintock. Anyway, it wasn't
possible to stay away from them completely. You know
how it is with family.''

Actually, Cole didn't know how it was. He'd had little
experience with family life.

She twisted around to look up at him, and he noticed
that a strand of her pale blond hair had escaped the barrette
that held it back, to fall over her forehead. He resisted the
urge to gently brush it to one side.

''The worst part was when I'd run across Randy when
Sheila wasn't around. Even though he was married, he—
he wouldn't leave me alone.''

The memory of some of what he'd overheard that morning when he'd been trapped in that back room at the community center told Cole she wasn't exaggerating the
situation.

*. . . There's no reason why we can't take up where we
left off,* the arrogant so-and-so had said, and *There are ways
we can meet without Sheila finding out . . .* Cole's hands
balled into fists.

''Sheila could see what was going on, of course, and she
blamed me. Or at least she pretended to. I think she must
have known the truth, but she never would have admitted
she'd made a big mistake in marrying Randy. By then it
was no secret that their marriage was in trouble—they'd

already had several arguments in public. Aunt Nadine had been dropping hints around town that I was the cause of their problems, that I still wanted Randy. Nothing could have been farther from the truth. I wouldn't have him on a silver platter.''

Although her tone was matter-of-fact, Cole didn't miss a slight catch in her voice. He felt a need to touch her, to communicate his sympathy in some way. He started to raise his arm to put a hand on her shoulder, then thought better of it. ''People didn't actually believe you were still interested in him, did they?'' he asked.

''Not at first—at least, I don't think they did. But then there was that accident—''

The accident that had left Randy with a permanent limp. Bits of gossip he'd heard, implicating Jamie, came back to him now, gossip he'd done his best to ignore. But that was before this sudden and surprising surge of protectiveness, so foreign to his nature, had overridden his usual caution about getting involved in other people's affairs. Since he *had* become involved, he felt he couldn't back out now. ''What exactly did happen?'' he asked.

She took a sip of her now cold coffee, then made a face. She looked around for a spot to put down the coffee mug. Cole took it from her and set it on an end table.

''I had to go to a teachers' meeting one evening, and Dad asked me to stop by the Cattlemen's Hall as long as I was in town, and drop off some papers for him. He was president of the local Cattlemen's Association at the time,'' she explained. ''There was a dance going on there—the town used to hold a dance at the Cattlemen's Hall once a month.''

She drew a shaky breath. ''Randy and Sheila were at the dance, and they'd been arguing. I'm not sure what it was about, but Randy had had too much to drink, and Sheila had been flirting with some cowboy from a ranch over near Alden. I'd hoped I could just drop the papers off and leave without being drawn into it, but when I went out to my car, I found they'd moved their argument to the parking lot.''

Cole's instinct told him not to say anything, to just let her tell the story in her own time.

"Randy wanted to leave, and Sheila was trying to get the car keys away from him. When he wouldn't let her have them, she yelled at him to go ahead and kill himself if he wanted to. She said she'd be glad to be rid of him. Then she stormed back inside in a huff.''

She paused briefly before going on. "I wanted to just drive off and not have to even think about Randy and Sheila and their problems, but—well, when I saw him trying to unlock his car, and I could tell he was so drunk he could hardly fit the key into the lock, I had to do *something*. It had started to rain, and I knew the roads would be bad. I tried to talk him out of trying to drive, but the only way I could keep him from it was to tell him I'd take him home.''

Cole could picture her trying to reason with a drunken, belligerent Randy. He realized his jaw was tightly clenched. "Wasn't there anybody else who could have looked after him?" he asked.

Jamie shook her head. "I was the only one around, and I was afraid if I went back inside to get help, he'd be gone by the time I got back. He was determined to leave right then, and I knew if I let him get behind the wheel of the car, he'd be likely to kill himself.''

Cole bit back the *Good riddance* that sprung to his lips. He knew that same sense of duty that would send her over here to tend to the injury of a old grouch like himself would also keep her from allowing Randy to drive while drunk.

"He and Sheila were staying out at her folks' place, and it was a long drive on dark, winding country roads. Once we got out of town, Randy wanted me to take him out to the County Line Tavern. When I wouldn't do it, he grabbed the steering wheel away from me. I tried to fight him off, but the roads were muddy, and the car started sliding. Before I could regain control, we went over the embankment—"

Her voice broke, and Cole noticed her hands were shaking. He wanted to take her in his arms, to hold and comfort her. He knew, though, that if he touched her at all, he wouldn't want to let her go. Instead, he said briskly, "How about some more coffee?"

"Coffee?" she echoed vaguely. "Oh—yes, I'd like some."

Picking up both coffee mugs, he went into the kitchen. He took his time about rinsing them out and refilling them. By the time he returned, she seemed to have regained her composure. She accepted the mug he held out to her and took several sips from it before she continued her story.

"I woke up in the hospital three days later. I'd been buckled in, so I came through it with just a concussion. Randy wasn't so lucky. He'd been thrown from the car.

Although she spoke in a dispassionate, impersonal voice, as if she were relating something that had happened to another person, Cole suspected she wasn't as detached as she pretended to be. It was a tactic he had often used himself, to keep others at bay.

"I wanted to go home, but the doctors insisted I stay in the hospital a few more days, for 'observation.' I was a little surprised that I didn't have more visitors while I was there. And the people who did come by seemed uncomfortable around me. I didn't understand what was going on until my folks broke it to me."

She turned toward the window. The only sounds were the rain, and a soft, whoosing noise as a log in the fireplace broke in two.

Cole busied himself stoking the fire before coming back to stand behind Jamie. "And . . ." he prompted gently.

Her wistful sigh touched something deep inside him. "It seems that Sheila and her cowboy had been the first on the scene. They'd followed us. I suppose she was hoping to catch us in a compromising situation. She was the one who gave a statement to the sheriff about what had happened, since I was unconscious and Randy was in no condition to tell them anything. Naturally, she twisted everything around. According to her story, there was—well, something going on between Randy and me. When she'd spotted us leaving together, she and her cowboy had followed us in his car because she was 'worried' about us—"

She broke off as a peal of thunder shook the house. Cole was standing close enough to her that he could feel her trembling. When the storm had begun this afternoon, he'd been a little surprised at the sudden fear she hadn't been able to hide. She hadn't struck him as someone who would be afraid of thunder and lightning. Now he understood.

Throwing caution to the wind this time, he put a hand on her shoulder. He held his breath, wondering if she might stiffen at his touch, or even shrug off his hand. Instead, almost as if she were unaware of what she was doing, she reached up and placed her own hand over his. He released his breath slowly.

"By the time I regained consciousness, the damage had been done," Jamie continued when the last rumble had died away. "Sheila's version of what happened was all over town. I couldn't go around buttonholing people and making them listen to the real story. I thought the whole thing would blow over in time, but—'' Her shrug spoke volumes.

Cole understood, from bitter experience, the futility of trying to defend oneself against unfounded accusations. ''Is that when you decided to go away?''

She removed her hand from his, as if she'd just realized it was there. Cole took his own hand from her shoulder and let it drop to his side.

The silence in the room lengthened. Just when Cole was beginning to think she wasn't going to reply, she said, ''No, that wasn't it. I was prepared to stick it out. I knew I hadn't done anything wrong. But then a delegation from the school board came to call. I'd been teaching fourth grade at McClintock Elementary, you know. They said that 'under the circumstances,' they'd understand if I'd rather not finish out my contract. They'd be willing to accept my resignation. It was a not very subtle way of saying they didn't think the children of McClintock should be exposed to someone with my reputation.'' Her voice was tinged with sarcasm.

Cole could feel the muscles in his jaw tighten. ''If you don't mind my asking, why was everyone so willing to put the blame on you instead of on Randy?''

She shrugged. ''It's that 'boys will be boys' mentality.'' Randy was a local hero. He'd been the big football star in high school, and folks were inclined to be tolerant of his occasional indiscretions. But I'd always been a 'pillar of respectability,' so I guess I was supposed to be above reproach. I like Caesar's wife.''

As she whirled to face Cole, her eyes glittered with remembered anger. ''When they asked for my resignation, that was when I decided to get away from here. Maybe it was cowardly, but I'd had about all I could take.''

''But you did come back. That took courage.''

Her lips twisted into a rueful expression. "Sometimes—like when I had that confrontation with Sheila and Randy at the community center, or that day in the hardware store when Roy Mayfield tried to pretend I'd turned invisible—I think I must have been out of my mind to return." She glanced down at her hands, her lowered lashes hiding her expression. When she looked up, her eyes met his. "By the way, I never did thank you for standing up for me."

Cole lifted one shoulder in a dismissive shrug. "Nothing to thank me for. I didn't like Roy's attitude."

"Anyway, I did appreciate what you did—even if I didn't show it," she said. "I know things like that are going to happen from time to time, and I'm trying to not let it get to me. This time I'm not going to let them drive me away."

He detected a touch of the bravado he'd noticed at other times. He wanted to offer some encouragement, to say, *Atta girl, stay in there and fight.* He was unaccustomed to putting his thoughts into words, though. He went over to the fireplace and tossed another log on the flames, watching as it sent up a shower of sparks.

In the silence that followed, Jamie found herself suddenly wishing she hadn't been so quick to air out the family skeletons. When he'd asked, "Want to talk about it?" she doubted that he'd expected to hear her life story.

"I—ah—I'd better be going," she said. "I'm sure you have things to do."

"You can't leave yet." He nodded toward the window. "It's still raining."

She followed his glance. "It looks like it's starting to let up." She didn't sound very convinced, though.

He stood with his hands on his hips, his eyebrows drawn together in a frown. Then, with an air of having made up his mind, he put a hand under her elbow and firmly guided her over to the sofa. ''There's no way you can drive in this kind of weather,'' he said, in a tone that brooked no argument. ''You might as well sit down and make yourself comfortable.'' With that, he turned to the fireplace and began repositioning the logs with the poker.

Jamie stared at his back in astonishment. She opened her mouth to protest at this domineering attitude, then closed it as she realized he wasn't being bossy, just sensible. And, although it went against her sense of independence to admit it, it was a relief to have the matter taken out of her hands, to be told what to do. Despite her attempts to take the storm in stride, she hadn't relished the idea of driving home in it. For just a second or two, she allowed herself to fantasize about what it would be like to have someone occasionally make a decision for her, to not always have to be strong and independent.

What was the point in rushing off, anyway? Did she honestly believe he was going to think any less of her now that he knew what people were saying about her? He didn't strike her as one who would be judgmental.

Besides, it had felt good to get the whole thing out in the open, to have someone willing to listen to *her* side of the story for once. She'd kept it hidden inside herself for too long. And he'd been a good listener, letting her tell it in her own way and in her own time, not rushing her, offering just the right touch of quiet sympathy.

Once the logs had been rearranged to his satisfaction, Cole stood up and glanced toward her, as if making sure she hadn't slipped out while his back was turned. Jamie detected a brief look of relief in his expression when he saw her sitting demurely on the sofa. She couldn't help wondering if he'd been worried about what he'd do if she'd insisted on starting home. Would he have felt duty-bound to forcibly restrain her? For some reason, the mental image of Cole putting his hands on her shoulders, gently but determinedly keeping her from leaving, didn't evoke the resentment she expected it to. In fact, the thought made her feel protected and cared for. It was a feeling she hadn't experienced in a long time.

Unexpectedly, a lump rose in her throat, and she found herself blinking back tears. She resisted the urge to wipe the back of her hand across her eyes. She couldn't let herself get all choked up just because her neighbor had had the good sense to talk her out of doing something potentially dangerous.

He was still standing next to the fireplace, half facing her, one arm resting on the mantel. With the firelight casting shadows across his features, his expression was closed, unreadable. It occurred to her that although she'd just told him things about herself she'd revealed to very few people, she still knew almost nothing about him. He was as much an enigma as the first time she'd set eyes on him.

After a moment of indecision, she asked, "What's *your* story?"

"What?" His remote expressison quickly changed to something close to alarm.

"I told you about what people are saying about me, and why. Why not tell me what the deep, dark secret is that *you've* been keeping bottled up."

"There's nothing to tell," he replied tersely.

He reminded her of a wild animal, wary of letting anyone get too close.

"Don't expect me to believe that. You're the town mystery man. Nobody knows a thing about you—where you're from, what you did before you came here . . ."

"I don't like bandying my personal business about."

Jamie felt a flash of irritation. "What was it you said? 'Sometimes it helps to get things out in the open.' Apparently that applies to everyone except you. Obviously, you're so supremely self-sufficient that you don't need anyone else. That's why you shut yourself away from the rest of the world.''

He opened his mouth as if to protest, but before he could say anything in his defense, she went on, ''If I'd known you were so far above the rest of us mere mortals, I'd have kept my own petty problems to myself. I'm sorry I bothered you.''

Cole hunched his shoulders and jammed his hands into his pockets. Noticing that he looked slightly ashamed, Jamie wondered if she might have made a dent in that stubborn reserve of his. She decided it was time to back off just a little. She didn't want to push too hard.

''It's not a pretty story,'' he said in a low voice that was almost a growl.

''And you're afraid it's too lurid for my delicate ears? Don't forget, I'm the town's scarlet woman.''

He considered this for a few moments, then gave a shrug, as if to say, *All right, lady, you asked for it.*

Chapter Twelve

"I didn't grow up in one of those 'traditional' families."

Cole said the word *traditional* with a touch of scorn. "I never knew my father but, from what I've been told, he started serving a term for armed robbery shortly before I was born." He glanced at Jamie, as if waiting for the look of horror to come over her features.

Jamie raised an eyebrow. "If you're trying to shock me, it isn't working. This isn't the dark ages. People aren't judged for what their parents do."

He was thrown somewhat off guard by her failure to be properly appalled at his revelation, but he recovered quickly. "There's more. If good old Dad was no prize, it seems Mom would never qualify for mother of the year either. She dumped me when I was about three. At that age, I was too old to be adoptable—most people want cute, cuddly babies—so I spent most of my childhood being passed from one institution or foster home to another."

Jamie bit off the words that sprang to her lips, knowing he would misinterpret any expression of sympathy as pity.

"Even among 'county kids' there was a hierarchy," he went on. "If you were orphaned, people felt sorry for you and were inclined to cut you a little slack. But if you were on the county because you'd been abandoned, or had a parent in prison, you were pretty far down on the totem pole. Since I qualified on both counts, that put me smack dab at the bottom of the pecking order."

It was easy to see how badly he was hurting—even after all these years—under that show of bravado. Jamie could picture him as a lonely, friendless child, being ostracized for things he had no control over. Still, she sensed there was more to the story. That alone wouldn't have made him so prickly, so afraid to allow anyone to get close to him.

"You said you spent *most* of your childhood in institutions and foster homes. Does that mean you eventually found a permanent home?"

The laugh that escaped him was bitter and mirthless. "Yeah, I found a permanent home all right—in the state correctional facility . . . Reform school," he translated.

"Do you intend to tell me what you were accused of, or are we going to play twenty questions?"

"I'll give you the short version. I got in with the wrong crowd of kids. I didn't know what they were up to when they robbed a warehouse. I know it sounds like a cop-out when I say I was an innocent bystander, but I swear it's the truth." At that moment, a flash of lightning outside the window illuminated his face, making the deep grooves on either side of his mouth more pronounced. "Anyway," he went on, "when the police drove up, they all scattered, and I was left holding the bag. You can believe that or not. It's up to you."

She met his defiant scowl without flinching. For several seconds their glances locked, until Jamie looked away. "Why wouldn't I believe it?"

"Why *would* you? Nobody else did."

"Apparently you've forgotten who you're talking to. I know what it's like to be the target of unfair accusations," she reminded him.

For just a moment, he looked almost ashamed, as if he had remembered she wasn't the enemy.

"So what happened then?" she prompted.

He turned away, looking into the fire. "Under normal circumstances, it would have been considered a minor offense, and I'd probably have gotten off with probation. But it seems my so-called 'friends' had been pretty busy. And since the police were convinced they had their man, I ended up taking the heat for a whole string of unsolved warehouse robberies. The juvenile court judge decided to make an example of me."

Although Jamie couldn't see his expression from this angle, she didn't miss the sudden tightening of his jaw.

"Wasn't there anyone who believed in your innocence?"

He gave a short, harsh laugh. "If there was, they kept mighty quiet about it. I didn't see anybody leaping to my defense. I guess everybody figured, 'like father, like son.' "

Jamie fought against an urge to go up behind him, wrap her arms around his waist and rest her cheek against his back, to try to take away that sense of aloneness he'd been carrying around all these years. But his entire being discouraged any display of sympathy.

She settled for a brief and, she knew, inadequate, "I'm sorry."

"Nothing to be sorry about." He turned to face her. "I'd never have gotten such a complete education if it hadn't been for that 'training facility.' There's nothing like a year or two in a place like that to teach survival skills.'' As he spoke, he was absentmindedly running one finger along the scar just below his eye. ''Of course, some lessons were harder to learn than others, but—well, you know what they say about experience being the best teacher.'' There was a bitter, mocking tone to his voice.

He shrugged off the momentary twinge of guilt he felt as he saw the way her eyes widened in—what? Shock? Hurt? So what if he'd offended her delicate sensibilities? She'd asked for it, hadn't she?

He knew he wasn't being fair, though. It wasn't her fault he'd had a rotten childhood, that he'd taken the punishment for others' misdeeds, that he'd learned early in life that trusting others only led to disappointment. He supposed he owed her an apology. Although that sort of thing didn't come easily to him, he knew when he was in the wrong. He was trying to find the right words, when it occurred to him that the expression on her face wasn't one of hurt or shock. He'd seen her eyes shoot out those jade green sparks a couple of times—when she was angry.

''Do you intend to go through life blaming everyone else for the things that happened to you?'' she demanded.

''I'm not—'' He stopped, as if aware there was more than a grain of truth in what she said.

''As you said, it's not a pretty story,'' she conceded. ''But Cole, it's all in the past. I'm not saying you didn't have a rough time, but isn't it time you let it go?''

Cole glared at her. ''Now listen, you were the one who insisted on hearing it all.''

''Because I thought it might do you some good to get it out in the open. I'd be willing to bet you've never told these things to another living soul. You're so wrapped up in your own bitterness you won't let anyone get close to you.'' She took a step toward him. ''You're—how old?''

Taken aback, Cole retreated until his back was against the fireplace brick. ''Almost forty,'' he mumbled, wondering what that had to do with anything.

''All those things took place more than twenty years ago, while you were still in your teens. It's time you put it behind you. You're a successful rancher. You've earned the acceptance of everyone around here. All the men like and respect you, and the women—'' Her voice trailed off as it occurred to her that she would rather not go into the matter of the effect he had on women. ''But you're so afraid of being hurt again that you've built this wall around yourself, and you won't let anyone in.''

Cole's expression was defiant. ''I found out it doesn't pay to let other people get too close.''

''So you're going to spend the rest of your life hiding behind that wall?'' she challenged.

He was getting a little tired of having to defend himself. ''You, of all people, should understand. You've lived here all your life. These people are *supposed* to be your friends. Yet ever since you came back here they've treated you like you have the plague.''

''But I did come back. And I faced up to whatever they had to dish out. I didn't shut myself away in some tower where I'd never have to be exposed to the risk of being hurt.''

Cole opened his mouth to protest, then closed it again as a montage of images played through his mind: the gossip he'd heard about Jamie that day in the diner; the episode in the hardware store when Roy Mayfield had acted as if she didn't exist. He was sure there had been other incidents that he hadn't witnessed. Not only that, but she'd also had to contend with her ex-fiancé trying to make passes at her, as well as her cousin's verbal abuse. If anyone had good reason to turn tail and run, she did. Yet she gave every indication that she intended to stick it out.

A twinge of self-reproach nagged at him as he looked down at the diminutive figure standing in front of him, her hands on her hips and her eyes blazing. All at once he couldn't think of a single thing to say in his defense.

He needed to put some distance between himself and Jamie. He placed his hands on her shoulders to move her back away from him a little. His original intention was forgotten as he felt the warmth of her skin, the delicate bone structure, through the thin material of her shirt. A wave of unexpected emotions took him by surprise. His instinct for self-preservation told him he should run from this situation as if his life depended on it.

Already, though, his nerves and muscles refused to do his bidding. Instead, his thumbs gently stroked the smooth skin at the base of her throat, making small circles. The ends of his fingers tingled from the contact.

He heard her little gasp of surprise and felt her soften beneath his touch, as if all the heated words of the last few moments were forgotten. She raised her eyes to his and several heartbeats of time thudded between them as their gazes clung.

The alarm going off in his head warned him that he was fast reaching the point of no return. With what little trace of rational thought he still possessed, he told himself he had to stop this before it got out of hand. And he had every intention of doing just that. Any second now.

But he knew it was already too late.

He pulled her nearer, letting his hands slip down until they were flat against her back. As she came to him without hesitation, as if this was exactly where she wanted to be, she gave a soft little sigh. It was that sigh that completely undid him.

Emotions he'd never before experienced were taking place inside him. He could almost feel the layers of ice melting around that part of his inner self he'd always kept aloof and inviolate. The surprising part was that he didn't mind. He didn't have that sense of caution, almost of foreboding, that usually overtook him when he sensed someone was getting too close.

Standing on tiptoe, she reached up and twined her arms around his neck, her soft curves molding themselves against the solid planes of his body. Their lips were just inches apart. It would take only the slightest movement . . .

When his mouth met hers, gently at first, then with an urgency that couldn't be denied, nothing had ever felt so right. His last trace of resistance went out the window.

Sanity returned with halting steps. Slowly, reluctantly, they drew apart. Time came to a sudden, jangling halt as he gazed down at her. With infinite gentleness, he reached out and brushed a stray tendril of hair away from her face.

Jamie stood perfectly still, hardly daring to move or even breathe. Whatever was happening between them was so fragile, so untouched, she was afraid if it wasn't handled gently, it might shatter like an iridescent bubble.

When Cole's fingers moved from her hair to trace an imaginary line down her cheek, she was sure her bones must be melting. Feeling an aching need to be closer to him, she untwined her arms from around his neck, wrapped them around his rib cage, and rested her cheek against his chest. She felt him tense up at first. Then he relaxed, and his arms came around her again, making her feel as if she were delicate—and infinitely precious.

They stood that way, neither of them saying anything,

for a long time, listening to the rain, the crackle of the fire, the synchronized beating of their hearts.

When Cole finally spoke, his voice was warm and husky, and tinged with awe. "I—I love you, you know."

She didn't have to be told that he'd never said those words to another living person. Something in her heart filled to overflowing at the knowledge. "I love you too," she whispered, glancing up at him through her lashes.

Holding her a little apart from him, he searched her face, as if hardly daring to believe what he was hearing, Then, slowly, like the sun coming out after the rain, he smiled down at her. It was the first time she'd seen a real smile on his face, not just a wry grimace, or a perfunctory curling of his lips. All at once, his entire countenance was transformed. The grooves alongside his mouth deepened, and interesting crinkles radiated from the corners of his eyes.

He took one of her hands in his and gently kissed her fingertips. Jamie wondered if he had any idea of what these light caresses were doing to her.

"Where do we go from here?" he asked.

Yes, where *did* they go from here, Jamie wondered, her emotions in a whirl.

This wasn't the first kiss they'd shared, of course. There was that night when he'd helped her bring Emmett home. But that had been just a giving in to a momentary weakness. This time, however, the electricity that had sprung up between them was more than a physical attraction. She sensed that some kind of invisible barrier had been let down. Oh, it wasn't anything either of them could *see*, but it had been there just the same, as substantial, and as inviolate, as a brick wall.

Common sense told her to proceed slowly, to think with her head and not her heart. What did common sense matter, though, when her lips still tingled from his kiss? But no matter what happened, she knew, beyond any doubt, that her life would never be the same again.

Where do we go from here? he'd asked. A few seconds stretched into an eternity as his eyes searched hers with unspoken questions. She swallowed. "I guess that's up to you."

"I—I'm kind of rusty at this sort of thing," he admitted, with a wry smile. "Maybe we'd better take things one day at a time."

She understood that he wasn't putting her off. He'd been shying away from emotional involvement for so long that he actually *didn't* know how to proceed. All at once she was filled with tenderness for this shy, lonely man who'd never learned to give or receive love. Standing on tiptoe, she gave in to the urge to kiss the pulse that was throbbing at the base of his throat. He looked surprised, but pleased.

"One day at a time," Jamie agreed.

She let Cole lead her over to the sofa. When they were seated, he drew her into his arms and pulled her so close that her head was resting against his shoulder. There was no need for words. A sort of silent communication flowed between them, as if their two souls were intertwined.

After a while, Jamie said, "Tell me about yourself."

He pulled away to look down at her. "I thought I already did. What else is there to tell?"

"You told me about your childhood, and your teenage years. I don't know a thing about what the rest of your life was like. Where are you from? How did you happen to become a rancher? What are your likes and dislikes?"

"You don't really want to hear about my life," he said. "It's not very interesting."

"I want to know all about you," she persisted.

He gave a little shrug. "I was raised up around Seattle. After I finished my—ah—my term in the correctional facility, I decided to get away from that area. Too many memories. I did a stint in the Army. Since my so-called offense took place while I was a minor, the records were sealed when I turned eighteen. Otherwise, the military probably wouldn't have taken me,'' he explained.

"After my hitch in the Army was up, I bummed around the country, working at different jobs—whatever came my way. I did a little of everything, from logging to digging ditches. Eventually I ended up on a cattle ranch in Montana. That was when I began to think I'd like to spend my life as a rancher. I liked the solitude—and I liked the idea of being my own boss. I knew if I ever planned on having my own spread, I'd have to strike out on my own, so I went back to Washington and managed to get on at Boeing. After working on a ranch, I hated having an indoor job, but the pay was good. For a couple of years, I socked away every cent I could spare. I was beginning to think I'd never have enough to buy my own place, though. Then I got a letter from a lawyer, telling me an uncle of mine—my mother's brother—had died, and I was his only heir. There were some papers enclosed that I was to sign so that my inheritance could be released."

He gave a wry laugh. "I didn't even know I had an uncle, let alone one with anything to leave me—although I expected it to be something like his watch, or maybe a few family pictures. I don't even know how the lawyer managed to locate me. I guess he started with my Army records."

"Will you get to the point?" Jamie said impatiently, aiming a playful punch at his arm. "What was the inheritance?"

"Oh. Well, even though it wasn't enough to make me rich, it was more than I'd expected. Added to what I'd already saved, it was enough to make a down payment on a ranch. I heard about this place in Oregon that was for sale, so I came down here to take a look at it. I liked what I saw, so I bought it.'' He shrugged. ''That's pretty much the whole story.''

''No one could ever accuse you of talking about yourself too much,'' Jamie murmured.

''What?''

''Oh, nothing.'' She had a feeling he'd gradually want to open up to her without being prodded, to share more of his thoughts and feelings.

''Now it's your turn,'' he said.

''My turn?''

''Uh-huh. What kind of little girl were you? Did you play with dolls? Ride horses? What were you like as a teenager?''

She was silent for several moments as she thought this over. A multitude of images passed through her mind, of growing up in a home filled with love, of having parents who'd always been there when she'd needed them. Sometimes she missed her mother and dad so much it was almost a physical pain. How she wished she could regain those five years she'd spent away from McClintock. If she'd had any inkling she was going to lose her parents so soon . . .

But it was too late for regrets. Nothing could change the past. Besides—unlike Cole—she at least had pleasant memories of her growing-up years to look back on.

She swallowed the lump in her throat. ''I guess I had a pretty normal childhood. I don't recall spending a lot of time playing with dolls. My tastes ran more to riding horses and helping Dad with ranch chores. And in high school I wasn't much interested in being head cheerleader or homecoming queen. I left that sort of thing to my cousin Sheila, who loved being the center of attention. I did edit the

school paper my senior year." She gave a little shrug. "I
can't think of anything else you'd be interested in."

Cole raised an eyebrow. "That's it?" he teased gently.
"Your entire life in a few brief sentences? And *I've* been
accused of being closemouthed?"

"I don't really know what else to tell you. Except for
one notable incident—which you already know about—
I've led a very uneventful life."

"Boyfriends?" he asked. Unless all the guys in
McClintock were blind, or just plain stupid, they must have
flocked around her like bees around honey, he thought.

She lifted one slender shoulder in a shrug. "I guess I
had my share in high school. I wasn't really the belle of
the ball type, though. I was too tomboyish. And I dated
some in college, of course, but nothing serious. It wasn't
until I finished college and came back here to teach that
Randy began paying attention to me."

Her green eyes clouded over. "I guess I was flattered.
He'd never noticed me back in high school. I can hardly
believe I didn't realize what he was really like, but—well,
I'm afraid I wasn't too worldly."

Cole sensed she'd led a relatively sheltered life, sur-
rounded by people who'd loved and protected her. She'd
have been completely out of her league with someone like
Randy. Even now, after all that had happened, there was
still a sort of childlike naïveté about her, so that she was
caught off guard when others failed to live up to the accepted standard of decent behavior.

He felt a surge of anger toward Mayfield for all he'd
done to destroy that naïveté; toward Sheila for blaming
Jamie for the problems in her own marriage; toward all the
townsfolk who were willing to believe the worst about her.

His thoughts were interrupted by the sound of the back

door opening, accompanied by Levi's, "Hey Boss, we gonna finish setting them fence posts?"

Jamie blinked in surprise as she glanced at the window. She saw that the sky had cleared up and the clouds were parting, revealing patches of blue sky. She began to smooth her disarranged hair back into place.

With a groan, Cole reluctantly released her. "I'll be right out," he called to Levi. He brushed a light kiss across Jamie's lips. Then, as if aware that that wouldn't be anywhere near enough to sustain him, he pulled her into his arms for one last embrace. Their kiss was interrupted by Levi's impatient, "Hey, time's awastin'."

"I'll be seeing you," Cole whispered. "Soon."

By the time she accompanied him to the kitchen, where Levi waited just inside the door, Jamie had managed to achieve a cool, composed demeanor. The only indication that anything out of the ordinary might have taken place was the high color in her cheeks.

Still, Levi gave both of them a curious look as they filed past him. Although he refrained from comment, there was a knowing twinkle in his eye.

Chapter Thirteen

"I must say, you certainly have a glow about you," Val commented. She was sitting in a corner of the sofa in Jamie's living room, her feet curled up under her. She leaned forward to scrutinize Jamie. "Have you discovered some new kind of beauty treatment? Whatever it is, I hope you'll share it with me."

Jamie avoided meeting Val's eyes as she toyed with her coffee cup. She debated about whether to confide yesterday's events to the foreman's wife. What had taken place between her and Cole was so new and fragile—like a seedling just starting to push its way through the soil to reach the sunlight—that she wanted to keep it to herself for a while longer.

Besides, it had all happened so quickly, she was still having trouble believing it. As she looked back on the episode, it had a dreamlike quality, like something she had conjured up in her imagination.

What was there to tell, anyway? They hadn't actually

made any kind of commitment to one another. *I'll see you soon,* he'd said. What exactly did that mean? That he'd see her in a few days? A few weeks?

Or, it suddenly occurred to her, was he perhaps already having second thoughts about what had taken place yesterday? In the warm circle of his embrace, she'd had no reason to doubt his sincerity. Now, however, she couldn't help wondering if, after having spent a lifetime avoiding any kind of emotional involvement, he might be regretting having let down his guard. The thought sent a pang of emptiness through her.

The memory of the moments she'd spent in Cole's arms, of his declaration of love, was like a beautiful dream. She hoped it wasn't going to fade away, the way dreams do.

She realized Val was watching her, waiting for a response. "If I look any different, it's probably just because of all the ranch work I've been doing since I moved back here," she replied lightly. "I think it's known as 'that healthy, outdoorsy' look."

Val gave her a speculative glance. "If I didn't know better, I'd almost think you were in lo—"

Her words were interrupted by a light tap at the back door, which had been left open. This was followed by an uncertain, "Jamie? You there?"

Val's eyebrows shot up as she mouthed, "Cole Wyatt?"

Jamie nodded. She could feel her cheeks turning pink. "Come on in," she called out. "I'll be right there." To Val, she whispered, "Don't go away."

"Wild horses couldn't drag me away," Val replied.

When Jamie went into the kitchen, she found Cole standing just inside the door. She almost went weak at the sight of him. He looked so good in the faded jeans that emphasized his lean hips, and the flannel shirt that followed the lines of his trim torso and flat midriff. Something in her contracted at the memory of how it had felt to be held against that masculine body.

"I—ah—need to talk to you." He took his hat off and toyed with the brim.

The thought struck Jamie that maybe he had come by to tell her to forget everything that had happened yesterday, that it had all been a mistake. She looked into his eyes, almost afraid of what she'd see there.

"You know, the square dance is tomorrow night," he said.

She nodded. Everyone knew about the square dance. It was the highlight of the Oregon Trail Days celebration.

"I've never been much for going to dances," Cole went on, "but Dan Reynolds asked me to be there to help keep things running smoothly—because I'm on the committee." His lips twisted into a wry grin. "I don't know what made Dan think I'd be any good at overseeing a dance—" He shrugged self-consciously. "Since I—ah—have to be there, I was wondering if maybe you'd—ah—want to go with me."

Although it might not have been the most eloquent invitation in the world, Jamie went almost limp with relief.

"I'd love to!" she exclaimed. She hoped she didn't sound too eager, but she sensed that Cole wasn't into game-playing, any more than she was. Especially after yesterday, when they had bared their hearts and souls to one another.

"Good." He hesitated before going on, looking somewhat uncomfortable. "There's—ah—one thing you ought to know. I guess I should have told you before you said you'd go with me. So you could say no if you wanted to . . ."

What was he getting at, she wondered.

"The thing is—I don't square dance. I can fake my way through a slow dance, but when it comes to something that requires fancy footwork, like square dancing, I'm afraid I don't know a do-si-do from a left allemande . . .''

"It's all right," Jamie assured him. She knew the small combo that played for all the local functions always included a few "regular" numbers in their repertoire, for when the square dancers were getting tired and everyone was ready for a change of pace. Although she loved to square dance, she consoled herself with the thought that slow dancing, with Cole's arms around her and her head resting against his chest, would be infinitely more pleasant.

"I'll pick you up about seven," he said, shifting his weight to his other leg. "I'd better go now. I've got some tractor parts out in the truck that Levi is waiting for."

He made no move to leave, though. He took a few steps into the kitchen, until he was standing directly in front of her. Jamie looked up into his eyes, and her breath caught in her throat at the love she saw there.

He gently grasped her shoulders as he bent his head to brush his lips across hers. Although it was the lightest, tenderest kiss imaginable, it set all her senses on fire.

"I love you," he whispered. Then he was gone, leaving her with the feeling she'd imagined the brief episode.

But if she had imagined it, her lips wouldn't be tingling that way. A dreamy little smile played around her mouth as she returned to the living room.

Val didn't bother to move away from the door, where it was obvious she'd been eavesdropping. "What's going on between you and Cole?" she asked with unashamed curiosity.

"He—he asked me to go to the square dance with him," Jamie replied, striving to keep her voice and manner casual.

Val raised her eyebrows. "Oh?" The single word held a weath of meaning.

"He—he has to be there because he's on the committee. And since he has to drive right past here anyway—"

"Oh. Of course. He has to drive right past here."

Jamie noticed that her friend had tactfully refrained from reminding her that just a few days ago she had turned down Val's suggestion that she ride along to the dance with her and TJ. Although she knew the offer was well meant, she had told Val she wasn't quite ready to start attending social events.

That was the truth—at the time. Still smarting from the cool treatment she'd received from some of the townsfolk, she had no intention of exposing her poor, battered emotions to any more hurt.

"It's time you got yourself back into circulation," Val had prodded.

"I—I don't want to face all those people."

"Why not?" Val demanded. "You have a lot of friends in McClintock, you know."

"Oh? I haven't noticed them beating a path to my door to welcome me back," Jamie couldn't resist pointing out. She'd been unable to keep a slight touch of bitterness from her voice.

Now, however, she was seeing everything in a new light. The love she felt for Cole was so radiant and effervescent that it spilled over, touching everything around her with a golden glow.

The role of recluse had been foreign to her naturally outgoing nature. It was time to start the healing process, and that meant putting aside past hurts. If the people of McClintock were ready to meet her halfway, she was more than willing to let bygones be bygones.

"Hey, if you're going to that dance, we have to find you something to wear!" said Val. She grabbed Jamie's hand and pulled her into the bedroom.

"Don't you have anything with pizzazz?" she asked, rifling through the contents of the closet.

"Pizzazz?" Jamie echoed vaguely.

"You know—" Val broke off, as she found exactly what she was looking for. "Aha!" she exclaimed triumphantly, pulling out a simple, full-skirted peasant-style garment in a light blue cotton, with elastic around the top of the bodice so it could be worn off the shoulders. Holding it up against Jamie, she surveyed it critically. "Perfect," she pronounced. "You'll knock 'em dead."

Jamie wasn't sure "knocking 'em dead" was exactly the effect she was looking for. "I—ah—don't want to draw too much attention to myself," she admitted. Despite the mellow, forgiving mood she was in, she wasn't sure what kind of reception she could expect.

"Nonsense. Of course you want to draw attention to yourself. That's the whole idea. This is your reentry into local society. You might as well jump in with both feet instead of tiptoeing up and sticking one toe into the water. Now then," she went on, returning to the matter of Jamie's attire, "you'll need white sandals to go with the dress. Oh, and gold jewelry . . ."

Cole gave a relieved sigh as he headed home. He'd felt a sense of panic when Dan Reynolds had asked him to oversee the upcoming dance. As a committee member, there hadn't been any way he could gracefully refuse. It would look as if he was shirking his duty.

He'd fought an inner battle with himself before asking Jamie to go with him. He knew if they showed up together, everyone there would be watching them, wondering, conjecturing. He'd feel as if they were on display. Since he *had* to go to this dance, though, the whole thing would be easier on him with Jamie by his side.

His smiled wryly. He was supposed to be past the age of needing a security blanket. Still, he couldn't deny he'd be glad to have her there with him, even though he'd hoped their first date would be a little more private.

Actually, he found this whole prospect of dating somewhat intimidating, but he realized it was all part of the game. After yesterday's interlude, he'd allowed himself to think about what it would be like to be married to Jamie, maybe even eventually to have a family—ideas that, up to now, had been completely foreign to him. This was something he'd never expected to happen to him, and he was still awestruck with the wonder of it. He'd never had anyone of his own, and the thought gave him a warm, comfortable feeling.

He realized he was rushing things. They hadn't even talked marriage, or what the future held for them. *One day at a time . . .* they had decided yesterday.

Still, when they'd parted there had been a tacit, unspoken promise between them—as if they were both aware that there was no turning back. For the rest of eternity, their lives, their very souls, were irrevocably bound together. Now, after having had twenty-four hours in which to get used to the idea of being in love, he knew that what he wanted to do was whisk Jamie off to a minister and make her completely, irrevocably his.

That wouldn't be fair to her, though. She had a right to expect a proper courtship. And that meant going out to dances, dinner, movies, even though everything in him shrank from exposing their newly discovered love to public view.

Jamie twisted around so she could see her reflection in the full-length mirror from all angles. Val had made a good choice. The dress was flattering. The full skirt emphasized her slender waist, and the color made her eyes a sort of green-blue.

When Cole arrived to pick her up, the admiring gleam in his eyes told her her efforts had been worthwhile. It crossed her mind that Cole was looking pretty good himself. He was wearing the usual male attire for affairs of this sort—jeans and a western shirt—but his jeans were newer than the ones he wore for everyday, and his white shirt, open at the neck, accentuated his deep tan. Jamie noticed also that his boots had been polished until they shone. He looked masculine and handsome.

All at once a stab of panic ran through her. Yesterday, during the rainstorm, she had felt so close to him. Now, as she looked up at his tall form, he seemed almost a stranger.

Then she caught the expression in his eyes. It was . . . tender. Gentle. Loving. Wordlessly, he reached out and drew her to him. At first she was hesitant, but as his lips caressed hers, the last of her reserve evaporated. This was where she belonged.

Still, on the ride into town she couldn't control the butterflies in her stomach. Despite her new, softened outlook, she wondered what she was getting herself into. As Val had pointed out, this would be her reentry into local society. People would be watching her, wondering about her. And the fact that she was showing up with Cole, the local mystery man, would give them even more cause for speculation.

As if sensing her anxiety, Cole reached over and took her hand. "It'll be all right," he whispered. And all at once she felt it would be.

She was aware of the stares, and quite a few double takes, as she and Cole walked into the community center together. She would have seriously considered turning around and retreating into the darkness if it hadn't been for Cole's hand holding hers, giving her strength.

If some of the hellos were tentative, Warren and Marianne Eagleton's greeting more than made up for everyone else's lack of warmth. Marianne hugged her enthusiastically, and Warren pumped Cole's hand.

"I'm so glad you came, dear," Marianne said. She held Jamie at arm's length. "My, don't you look pretty. That dress is perfect for you." Some of the other guests took their cue from the Eagletons, and before long Jamie felt herself starting to relax.

Cole went about his duties—which included everything from changing burned-out lightbulbs to making sure the sound system was operating properly—in his usual calm, methodical manner, seemingly unaware that he and Jamie were the objects of so much interest and curiosity.

As the hall began to fill up, Herb Whittaker, who had been McClintock's official square dance caller for as long as Jamie could remember, stepped up on the stage. "Howdy, folks," he said into the microphone, in his deep voice. "As soon as Jake and his boys are finished tuning up we'll get this shindig started." He glanced over his shoulder at Jake Cooney and his Prairie Troubadours. "You fellows about ready?" At Jake's nod, he said, "Grab the prettiest gal you can find, and let's get down to some serious dancing."

Leaning against the wall, arms folded, Cole looked around the large room to see if there was anything else that needed his attention. As his glance took in the couples on the dance floor, it occurred to him that he and Jamie were almost the only ones not dancing. Even a perspiring Levi was whirling a plump, middle-aged woman through the steps of "Turkey in the Straw." He noticed the expression on Jamie's face as she watched the couples on the dance floor, and the way she instinctively tapped one foot in time to the music. For the first time in his life, he was sorry he'd never mastered the intricacies of square dancing.

It didn't escape Jamie's notice that many of the women were casting sidelong glances at Cole. Emily Dowling, from the library, who was presiding over the refreshment table, turned positively pink every time he stopped by for a sandwich or a glass of punch. And Billie Turner, the waitress at the Four Star Diner, sparkled like a Christmas tree whenever he was in the vicinity. Yet Cole seemed completely oblivious to the stir he was causing among the women of McClintock.

Jamie couldn't help smiling as she recalled Val's comment, "The man has absolutely no idea of the effect he has on women." With most men, this would be a pose, but in Cole's case, she knew he really hadn't a clue that women were practically drooling over him.

After several sets of squares, the small band swung into a lively rendition of "Achy Breaky Heart," and the dancers began to form into rows for country line dancing.

"Hey, why aren't you two out there?" a voice called out. Jamie glanced up to see Val heading straight for them, TJ in tow.

Cole shook his head. "I'm afraid dancing just isn't my thing."

Val brushed aside his protests. "Don't be silly. Anyone can line dance. You just keep doing the same steps over and over."

By the time Cole caught the determined look in her eye and realized her intent, it was too late to retreat. Putting a hand on Jamie's shoulder, he looked around for an escape route, but found their way blocked by TJ, who said cheerfully, "You might as well give in gracefully. Once my wife makes up her mind about something, there's not much point in arguing.''

"You can't bring a girl to a dance and then expect her to stand around on the sidelines all evening,'' Val said, easing her way in between Cole and Jamie. She linked one arm through Cole's and the other through Jamie's.

"I don't know how to do this,'' Cole protested.

Val waved away his resistance. "We'll teach you.''

"No, Val, please—'' Jamie began, but Val paid no more attention to her objections than she had to Cole's as she drew them off to a relatively uncrowded corner of the dance floor. Almost in a panic, Cole glanced at Jamie with an expression that clearly said, *Get us out of this*. He could see rescue wouldn't be coming from that quarter, though. She gave a little helpless, palms-up shrug.

"Now the first thing you need to learn is the Vine,'' Val said, demonstrating a step that struck him as being hopelessly complicated. "Try it.''

Cole felt utterly trapped. There was no way he could get out of this without drawing even more attention to himself and Jamie. Resigned, he tried to imitate the step Val had shown him, with Jamie's help. After a few false starts, he managed a passable version of the Vine.

"There, see how easy that was?'' Val said encouragingly. From there they progressed to the Stomp, the Bump, the Star, and the Kick.

Val gave his arm a reassuring pat. "You're doing great. Now all you have to do is put them together. Jamie will show you how.''

With that, she gave the two of them a little shove toward the center of the dance floor, where the line of dancers automatically separated to make room for them. Giving Cole an apologetic look, Jamie whispered, "I'm sorry about this.''

Although he hated feeling as if he were on display, he didn't want to give her the idea he blamed her. "Nothing to be sorry about," he assured her. "We'll muddle through somehow." He even managed a slight grin.

His brow furrowed as he concentrated on not tripping over his own feet. At least he was keeping up with the others, he thought, even though he wouldn't win any prizes for grace or style.

Eventually, he began to relax somewhat, as the sequence of the steps became more automatic. By the third or fourth repetition, he felt a little less awkward. A couple of times he glanced over at Jamie, and she smiled at him encouragingly.

She didn't seem to be having any problem keeping up with the other dancers, he noticed. Her steps were self-assured, her movements graceful and coordinated. She made such an attractive picture, with her fine, pale hair flying with each twist and turn, and her full skirt swirling gracefully around her slim legs, that his heart contracted in his chest.

He noted, with mixed emotions, that she appeared to be having the time of her life. He knew how apprehensive she'd been about coming to this dance. He was pleased— for her—that she was able to put that apprehension aside and enjoy herself.

Still, he couldn't suppress a pang of regret. Although he realized it was probably selfish of him, he would rather they were off by themselves in some private spot where they could shut out the rest of the world—a place where neither of them had to worry about being hurt by false accusations, where the spite and jealousy of others couldn't touch them. He wanted to protect her, to shield her.

He realized the fantasy of the two of them being together in their own secluded hideaway was just that—a fantasy.

No matter how badly he wanted to keep her all to himself, it wouldn't be fair to her. These were the people she'd grown up with, the people she'd known since childhood. Even though some of them had treated her shabbily, he knew she was willing to forgive and forget. It wouldn't be fair to expect her to shut out everyone else. She was entitled to a normal social life. It was her birthright.

And that was what was making him so uneasy. He'd seen what happened when you let your guard down and let other people get too close. You ended up getting hurt. True, nobody had made any untoward remarks to Jamie tonight—but that didn't mean all the good citizens of McClintock were ready to forget the gossip that had circulated around her.

His thoughts were interrupted by a muffled exclamation from someone behind him. He'd been so caught up in his musings that he'd forgotten to concentrate on his footwork, and had almost gotten tangled up with one of the other dancers. He could feel his face reddening as he made an effort to get back in step.

By the time the music ended, he felt as if he'd been fighting wildcats. As he escorted Jamie from the dance floor, she said, "I think I'd better go to the ladies' room and freshen up. I must be a mess by now." She tried to smooth her hair back into place with her hands.

"You look fine to me." Actually, he thought she looked a whole lot better than fine, with her cheeks flushed from the exertion and her hair slightly mussed.

The frank admiration in his eyes caused her to redden even more. "I'll be right back," she murmured, disengaging her hand from his. As he watched her walk away, he felt an elbow jabbing into his ribs.

"What—" He turned to see TJ grinning at him.

"You looked pretty good out there," TJ said. "I didn't know you had it in you."

Cole glared at him, but TJ remained cheerfully unintimidated. Cole turned and headed for the refreshment table, but before he got there he was approached by several more of the male guests, clapping him on the back and telling him how much they'd enjoyed his performance.

"Hey Twinkletoes," one cowboy called out, "how 'bout giving the rest of us some dancing lessons?"

Twinkletoes. Cole cringed. "I'll teach you a lesson," he growled. "But it won't be a dancing lesson."

They were getting a kick out of this, he realized. Everyone who knew him at all was aware of his dislike of drawing attention to himself, and now they couldn't resist having some fun at his expense. He knew their teasing was good-natured, but he wished they'd find some other way to amuse themselves.

Things didn't get any better when he got to the refreshment table. "You've been holding out on us," Billie commented, winking at him and rolling her eyes. "All this time you've been getting out of coming to dances by pretending you can't dance, but you had some pretty fancy moves out there on the dance floor."

This was too much, he thought. Turning on his heel, he strode away, just as Emily Dowling started to ask, "Won't you have some punch—" He headed toward the wide double doors that led to the entry hall, in search of Jamie. He was going to whisk her off to some quiet spot where they could escape all the teasing and the amused looks.

He gave a sigh of relief as the door to the ladies' room opened and Jamie emerged, her hair tamed back to its usual silky smoothness and her lips pink with freshly applied lipstick.

As she started across the entry hall, she was intercepted

by an older woman with a vaguely familiar look about her and an air of determination. The woman planted herself directly in front of Jamie.

Jamie took a step backward, a sudden expression of something like apprehension in her eyes. "Aunt Nadine—"

Aunt Nadine. Of course, Cole thought. He had the feeling she hadn't approached Jamie merely to chat about family matters.

Chapter Fourteen

Sensing trouble, Cole covered the distance between himself and Jamie in a few strides, and stood just behind her, in an attitude of protectiveness. As much as he wanted to shield her from whatever unpleasantness was coming, instinct told him to stay out of it unless she indicated she wanted his help. He settled for putting a hand on her shoulder in a gesture of support. "I'm here if you need me," he said under his breath.

"Thanks," she whispered back.

Nadine gave Cole a suspicious look, then returned her attention to Jamie. "You certainly made a spectacle of yourself out there," she began, without preamble.

Cole was taken aback by the venom in her voice. Apparently Jamie was too, judging by her quick intake of breath.

"I'd think you'd be ashamed to flaunt yourself that way," Nadine went on. "But then, you never did have any sense of decency."

Jamie looked as if she'd been struck. Cole felt a tremor run through her body.

Nadine pushed her face closer to Jamie's. "You're nothing but a man-chasing little tramp," she hissed. "You almost ruined my daughter's marriage by trying to steal her husband. If you'd stayed out of the way, Sheila and Randy would have been happy together."

Several people had stopped to see what was going on, when Nadine had begun her diatribe. At this last remark, there were audible gasps from some of the onlookers.

"Aunt Nadine, that's not true," Jamie said, finding her voice. "Randy and Sheila never got along from the day they were married. I had nothing to do with it. I wouldn't have Randy as a gift."

Nadine ignored Jamie's protests. "Then, to make things worse, you caused the accident that left Randy with that limp. It's all your fault that he's crippled."

"Now see here—" Cole put in, unable to hold his peace any longer.

"Cole, no," Jamie said under her breath. "Let me handle this."

"Are you sure?"

"I'm sure."

Although he wanted to make it clear to this obnoxious woman that she couldn't talk to Jamie that way, he yielded to her wishes.

She faced her aunt without flinching. "You know there was nothing going on between Randy and me. The only reason we were together that night was because he was so drunk I was afraid he'd kill himself or someone else if he tried to drive."

Nadine's only reply was a disbelieving sniff.

"I intended to drive him home, but once he was in my car he wanted me to take him out to the County Line

Tavern. When I refused, he tried to grab the steering wheel away from me. That's what caused the accident.''

''I see you're still sticking to that ridiculous story.'' Nadine tossed her head, oblivious to the small crowd that was gathering around them. ''Surely you don't expect anyone to believe you?''

Cole glanced around at the onlookers, who were taking in the proceedings with ghoulish interest. Wasn't there even one person in the bunch who was going to speak up in Jamie's defense?

As if reading his thoughts, Nadine's thin lips twisted into an expression of triumph. ''Nobody wants you here, Jamie. I don't know why you came back.''

At that, Frank Palmer, who had been watching from the doorway, approached his wife hesitantly. ''Now Nadine—'' he began in a placating tone. But when she fixed him with a frosty glare, he backed off.

''You should have just stayed away,'' Nadine hissed at Jamie.

Cole could feel Jamie stiffen. He leaned down so he could speak in her ear. ''You don't have to stay here and listen to this, you know.''

Jamie drew in her breath, then let it out slowly. ''You're right, I don't,'' she agreed after a moment of silence. Her head held high, she linked her arm through his and together they walked past the glaring Nadine, past her husband, who looked embarrassed and ashamed, past the goggle-eyed onlookers. The only indication she was upset was the color in her cheeks.

When they were back in the large main room of the community center, Cole's glance darted around them as he assessed the situation. It was obvious that most of the guests were unaware of the altercation that had taken place in the entry hall. He had no doubt, though, that in a matter of minutes, everyone would know.

"Now what?" he asked, leaving the next move up to her.

"Let's just get out of here."

"Right." He scanned the room, then quickly guided her to a side door, where they could make their exit without drawing too much attention to themselves.

Jamie's composure remained intact until they were inside Cole's pickup truck. Then, away from curious eyes, she gave in to the tears she had been holding back.

Seeing her this way was as painful to Cole as a knife tearing into his own flesh. All the hurts and injuries he'd suffered throughout his lifetime, all the little slights and the snide remarks about his background and parentage paled by comparison. He would willingly have endured them all, and more, in order to spare Jamie this humiliation. He was accustomed to abuse. He was tough, and could take it.

But Jamie—that was another story. Just the thought of her being subjected to this kind of persecution filled him with helpless rage. A sense of frustration welled up inside him. He didn't even have the words to comfort her. Feeling completely inadequate, he drew her into his arms and held her gently while she sobbed.

He'd had a feeling something like this might happen. He, of all people, knew how small-minded and suspicious people could be, always ready to think the worst of others. He blamed himself. He should have followed his instincts. If he hadn't asked her to come to this dinner with him.

But in the back of his mind he knew how ridiculous that was. He couldn't expect her to hide away. Still, he couldn't suppress a vague sense of guilt.

When they heard voices drawing near, Jamie pulled away from him and sat up straight, wiping her eyes with the back of her hand. There was no need to ask if she wanted to go back into the dance. He knew what her answer would be.

"Wait here just a minute," he said. "I'll be right back." Hurrying back into the community center, he buttonholed Walt Newly, a fellow committee member.

"Walt, something's come up and I have to leave," he said quickly. "I'd sure be obliged if you'd fill in for me."

"Well—sure. I guess so."

"Thanks. I was sure I could count on you." Handing the keys to Walt, he rushed off, tossing a quick, "Don't forget to lock up after everyone's gone," over his shoulder.

He and Jamie were silent during the ride home. When Cole pulled into Jamie's driveway, he turned off the ignition. "I'll come in with you."

"You don't have to—" she started to protest, but was silenced by the determined set of his jaw.

He went in the house ahead of her, turning on the kitchen light. With a light touch on her shoulder, he steered her into the living room, where he switched on a lamp in a corner of the room, but left the other lights off. Taking her hand, he sat down on the sofa and drew her down beside him. Then he put an arm around her and pulled her close, so that her head rested against his shoulder. He felt he could have held her that way forever, listening to her soft, even breathing, inhaling the clean, fresh scent that clung to her hair.

"I'd give anything if that business with your aunt hadn't happened," he murmured.

"I should have known she'd pull something like that, and tried a little harder to avoid her, but instead I walked right into it."

Cole crooked a finger under her chin and, with his

knuckle, tilted her face up to his. "Don't start blaming yourself. It wasn't your fault."

Although his tone and manner were matter-of-fact, he was seething inside at the memory of that scene back at the community center. One of the worst aspects of the whole thing—for him—had been having to stand off to one side and do nothing while that woman made cruel, untruthful accusations against Jamie. Wasn't it a man's duty to protect the woman he loved? But she'd made it clear she preferred to deal with this herself, and he'd felt duty-bound to respect her wishes. Most likely, she'd felt she had no right to involve him in her squabbles with her relatives. It wasn't as if they were married . . .

But if they *were*, he'd be in a better position to speak up in her defense the next time something like this happened—and he had no doubt it would.

That wasn't the only reason he wanted to marry her, of course, but it gave him the burst of courage he needed.

"You know I love you," he whispered, his voice low and husky. "Will you marry me?"

He'd never imagined himself saying those words to any woman. But he realized that what he wanted more than anything was to make Jamie his wife—to love her, to cherish her, to protect her.

His heart almost stopped beating when she drew away from him and glanced down at her hands. Was she going to tell him they were moving too fast, that they needed more time together before they could consider marriage?

Time hung suspended as he waited for her reply. It was impossible to tell what she was thinking. Her lowered lashes fanned out across her cheekbones, hiding her expression.

After what seemed an eternity, she looked up and her

glance met his. Even before she said, "Of course I'll marry you," the glow he saw in her eyes gave him his answer.

He hadn't realized he was holding his breath until it all came out in a rush. Now he felt almost light-headed with relief as it occurred to him that the rest of his life would be worth nothing without Jamie.

"We can drive down to Nevada—" he began.

"No."

At the soft monosyllable, his forehead creased into a perplexed frown. Had he misunderstood? "You just said—"

"When we get married, I don't want to sneak off as if we had something to hide. I'd like us to have a real wedding, right here in McClintock. In the church I grew up in. With a gown, flowers, and a wedding cake."

Cole was taken aback at the idea of the two of them being on display that way. He had a horrible vision of a repeat of the scene that had taken place at the dance happening at their wedding. But he made an effort to hide his dismay. After a few seconds of silence, he asked, "Do you really think having a big wedding is a good idea?"

"Of course. The best way to counteract all the gossip is to hold our heads up and let everyone know we have nothing to be ashamed of. Being in love is something to be celebrated, not hidden away."

Being in love . . . Something inside him contracted at the way she said it. Still, he couldn't shake the vague feeling that if that love were exposed to the narrow-minded, self-righteous people of McClintock, it would somehow become tarnished. He realized he'd have to proceed very carefully.

"And if we did have that kind of wedding, are you sure anyone would even come to it?" he asked.

"Oh, I have no doubt they'd come—out of curiosity, if for no other reason."

If that was meant to reassure him, it had exactly the

opposite effect. Everything in him shrank from being an object of curiosity.

As if reading his thoughts, Jamie went on, "Even if that was the only reason people came, I'm sure they'd start to soften once they got there. There's something about a wedding that brings out the best in folks."

"You make it sound as if they'd be doing us a favor by coming to our wedding. If they feel that way, why should we even bother?"

Pulling out of his embrace, Jamie tilted her head to one side and studied him. "We have to start somewhere. We want to be accepted by the people around here, don't we?"

Cole refrained from pointing out that he'd never cared much whether or not he was accepted by the people of McClintock, or anywhere else. "Why?" The single word came out sounding more brusque than he'd intended.

Jamie's eyes widened in surprise. "Why?" she echoed. "Well—because we all need other people. We can't just shut ourselves away from everyone, can we?"

"I've spent most of my life keeping my distance from others, and I've managed just fine," he pointed out.

"Well, I grew up with lots of friends," Jamie countered. "And I was involved in all the town functions and social affairs. I've missed that. I want things to be the way they used to be."

Cole could well imagine the kind of life she'd led before that one night had changed everything. As the daughter of one of the most successful and respected ranchers in the area, her position on the town's social scale had been assured.

And what had it gotten her, he wondered bitterly. "At the first hint of a scandal, all those so-called 'friends' turned their backs on you. Where were they tonight when your aunt was raking you over the coals? Did even one person offer you support? No, they all just stood there gaping.''

Jamie stood up and walked a few paces, as if to distance herself from Cole while she sorted out her thoughts. ''They—they would have. They were just taken by surprise.'' But her uncertain tone belied her words.

''Why don't you stop defending them!'' he burst out, rising to his feet. ''After the treatment you've received from the people in this town, why in heaven's name would you want to give them an opportunity to hurt you even more?''

Jamie picked up a small carved figure of a horse from the end table next to the sofa. She turned it over in her hands, studying it as if she'd never seen it before. ''Because I can't live in a vacuum,'' she replied, after several moments of silence. ''When I first came back, I was angry with everyone, and just wanted to be left alone.'' She replaced the figurine. ''It's not my nature to live that way. I need other people around me.''

''Well, I don't. All I need is you.'' Cole took a few steps toward Jamie, then stopped. He knew he couldn't think clearly if he was too close to her. Right now, he needed to be in full possession of his faculties, in order to make her understand. This wasn't just a minor disagreement. It was something that was going to affect their entire future together.

''That scene at the community center, with your aunt saying those things about you, and everyone else standing around taking it all in, just proved my point—that we'd be better off to keep to ourselves.''

''No. What it proved was that we just have to work a little harder at showing people that the things that are being said about me aren't true.''

"Why?" Cole forced a calm he didn't feel. "Why do we need anyone else in our lives?"

Her eyes averted, Jamie rearranged the knickknack on the table. Finally, when she seemed satisfied that they were in their proper positions, she looked up at him.

"If I thought you were serious, I'd be upset." A tentative smile played around the corners of her mouth.

Cole knew she wanted him to reassure her that he didn't mean the things he was saying. He couldn't mislead her, though. "I *am* serious."

The flat statement hung there in the air.

When Jamie finally spoke, her words were very clear and concise, as if she wanted to make sure she fully understood his position. "What you're telling me, then, is that when— *if*—we get married, you expect us to shut everyone else out of our lives?"

The word *if* was like a knife twisting inside him. Still, it was important that they get this settled. "I'm just saying I don't think it's a good idea to let other people get too close. When you start trusting people, you just let yourself in for a lot of disappointment."

There was another long silence, while Jamie considered this. Finally, she asked, "And if I don't agree to the kind of life you want for us?"

Jamie hardly dared breathe as she waited for his answer. The seconds ticked away into what seemed an eternity.

Cole shifted his weight uneasily. "I love you, Jamie," he said at last. "Do you have any idea what it does to me to see you treated the way you were tonight? All I'm asking is that you not put yourself in a position where that could happen again. Is that so wrong?"

"I can't live that way." There was a pleading note in Jamie's voice.

"And I can't live the way you want to—allowing other

people to get too close, giving them the chance to hurt us—"

Jamie drew a deep, ragged sigh. "I guess there's not much to say then, is there?"

For several seconds, as she waited for Cole's reply, the silence was almost a tangible thing. She felt as if she could reach out and touch it.

Cole raised his hands, palms up, in a gesture of helplessness, then let them drop to his sides. "I guess not." He turned and walked away.

As Jamie stared after his retreating back, every instinct in her longed to call him back, to reassure him that this was something they could work out. She felt frozen, however, too stunned to do anything except stand there mute while her hopes and dreams shattered into a million pieces.

She heard the back door open and close, with a soft little "click." There was a depressing finality in the sound.

Chapter Fifteen

Surely he'll come back, Jamie told herself. But that hope was dashed when she heard Cole's truck engine growling to life, followed closely by the crunch of tires on gravel.

She sank into an easy chair, curling her legs up beneath her and resting her cheek on the arm. What could have been seconds—or hours—ticked by as she huddled there, her brain numbed with shock.

Eventually, she was jolted out of her lethargy by a sudden clap of thunder. If a storm was coming up, she supposed she ought to go out to the barn to check on the animals and make sure everything was closed up tight. She went into the bedroom to change into her jeans.

As she replaced the blue dress, now wrinkled and limp, on its hanger, she couldn't help recalling how happy she'd been a few hours earlier, getting ready to go out with Cole. So much had happened since then. It seemed a lifetime ago that he had asked her to marry him, and she'd accepted.

That must have been the shortest engagement on record,

she thought wryly. She told herself how fortunate she was to have discovered, before she made the mistake of marrying him, how stubborn and unyielding he could be.

But the thought failed to give her any comfort.

Rather than going home by the road that ran between Jamie's ranch and his, Cole had taken the roundabout route. It took all his concentration to negotiate the winding back roads in the dark, leaving him no time to think about the scene that had just taken place.

Sooner or later he was going to have to take it out and look at it, but he wasn't quite ready yet. He pushed the whole incident to the back of his mind as he peered through the windshield into the blackness, straining to see the roadway in front of him.

Still, he couldn't continue driving around all night, he thought, scowling. It looked as if they might be in for a storm, anyway. He'd noticed a few brief flashes of quicksilver in the sky. They might be nothing more than heat lightning, but if it did rain, he didn't want to be caught out in it.

As he rounded the last curve in the road, the Lucky Horseshoe came into view. For once, the sight of the sturdy old ranch house failed to give him a sense of satisfaction.

Ever since he'd moved here, the rambling structure, with its stone front and weathered wood, had been a sort of sanctuary, a fortress where he could shut out the rest of the world. Now it just struck him as looking depressingly empty and barren, devoid of any welcoming warmth.

For the past few days, he'd allowed himself to imagine Jamie in his home, brightening every room with her presence, putting her own indelible stamp on the place. The simple word, *home,* had taken on a whole new dimension.

Now, it occurred to him that his ''fortress'' was nothing

but a pile of wood and stone. What good was a sanctuary without anyone—without Jamie, he amended—to share it with? All at once the rest of his life stretched out ahead of him in a bleak succession of monotonous days and lonely nights.

When he stepped into the house, the emptiness hit him like a physical blow. He strode through the rooms flipping on light switches, hoping the illumination would chase away the forlorn, desolate feeling.

Why couldn't Jamie have been reasonable about this, he wondered? It wasn't as if he was asking her to become a hermit. He'd only suggested they not go out of their way to be right in the middle of everything that took place in McClintock. She'd have them going to every party, every potluck and church social that came along.

And that spelled trouble.

Hadn't he learned the hard way that it didn't pay to allow people to get too close? Oh, for a while folks might make a show of welcoming her back into their circle, but sooner or later the old gossip would resurface. Somebody with a malicious streak would make some hurtful remark that would open old wounds. Why couldn't she understand that he just wanted to protect her from that sort of thing?

As Jamie stepped outside, the air felt thick and heavy—oppressive—as though mirroring her own mood. Scanning the sky briefly, she caught a quick flicker of light out of the corner of her eye.

Usually she found the barn a comforting place. The soft nickers that greeted her, the sweet-tangy scent of hay mingled with the pungent livestock aroma, the soft rustling of animals in their stalls, were all part of the familiar pattern that went all the way back to her childhood.

Tonight, though, the atmosphere inside the barn was anything but peaceful. A sense of foreboding—almost of impending doom—hung in the air. She told herself she was imagining things. It was just the threatening storm that was making her jittery. *Impending doom.* Hah! She'd been watching too many old movies on television.

That didn't explain the way the animals moved restlessly in their stalls, though, as if they too knew something was amiss.

She moved through the barn, checking to see that everything was in order, taking time to murmur a few words to the horses that poked their noses over the half doors of their stalls.

"There you are, darlin'."

Jamie gave a start at the sound of the voice behind her. Whirling around, she found herself facing Randy Mayfield.

"I stopped up at the house, but nobody seemed to be around," he said, as casually as if it was perfectly normal for him to drop by. "I thought you might be out here."

"What are you doing here?" she demanded. A visit from her ex-fiancé was all she needed to put the finishing touch on an evening that was already going steadily downhill. She found everything about him irritating, from his nonchalant slouch to the slightly glazed eyes and slurred tone that indicated he'd been drinking.

"I just thought I'd come by to see how you're doing." He tried to inject a note of hurt surprise into his words, as if he couldn't imagine why she wasn't delighted to see him. Jamie knew better than to be taken in by his guileless manner, though. She tapped one booted toe on the floor as she glared at him, waiting to see what he was up to.

He drew a cigarette from his shirt pocket. "Heard you had a little run-in with my mother-in-law tonight. Sweet old gal, isn't she? If I'd known—" He paused to light the cigarette. "If I'd known what I was getting into when I married into *that* family, I'd have given it a little more thought.''

Jamie refrained from pointing out the fact that being engaged to *her* at the time should have been adequate justification for further thought. ''Don't smoke in my barn,'' she snapped.

Randy took several deep drags of the cigarette before dropping it to the floor and grinding it out with his heel.

''What do you want, Randy?'' Jamie asked wearily.

He took a step toward her. ''I realize now what a mistake I made by marrying Sheila.'' His voice took on a plaintive, humble tone. ''You were the one I really loved.''

''Why don't you just leave?'' Jamie's words were flat, expressionless. ''Go home to your wife.''

Randy seemed momentarily taken aback, as if he were surprised that his ''sincerity'' wasn't getting through to her. He recovered quickly, however. ''It doesn't have to be over between us, you know,'' he said, moving closer to her.

She took a step backwards, coming up against the rough wood of the wall. Randy put an arm on either side of her and placed his hands against the wall, caging her in. He lowered his head so that his lips were very close to hers. ''We had something really great between us,'' he whispered.

Jamie's first thought was to call for help, until she remembered there was nobody around to come to her aid. The bunkhouse was too far away for anyone to hear her. Besides, most of the ranch hands were likely out for the evening, this being Saturday night. She was strictly on her own.

Her initial panic was quickly replaced by a surge of white-hot anger. Summoning a burst of strength she didn't know she had, she put her hands on Randy's chest and pushed with all her might.

The element of surprise was on her side and, caught off guard, Randy stumbled back a few steps. Blinking his eyes in astonishment, he fumbled in his pocket for a cigarette.

"Don't *ever* try anything like that again." Her eyes shot green sparks. "And I told you not to smoke in here," she flung over her shoulder as she strode from the barn.

Despite her show of bravado, she was trembling by the time she got to the house. Although she almost never locked her doors, she slid the bolt shut behind her as she slipped inside, then hurried to the front door and did the same. A few minutes later, she gave a sigh of relief as she glanced out the window and saw Randy's car squeal out of the driveway, spraying gravel.

She felt completely drained, as if she had no inner resources left. Instinctively, she headed for the phone to call Cole. She needed to draw on his calm, reassuring strength. But then she remembered that she had no right to turn to him for comfort. He'd made his feelings very clear when he'd walked out of her house.

And out of her life.

All at once she began to realize what a monumental mistake she'd made. She found herself wishing it was possible to take back the last hour or so and relive it. If she could, she would tell Cole that she'd gladly live with him in a cave, or on a deserted island, if that's what he wanted. What did it matter, as long as they were together?

It was too late, though. She'd thrown away the kind of love many people never find in a lifetime of searching.

All at once, she felt incredibly weary. Going into her bedroom, she threw herself across the bed, face down.

For an hour or so, Cole had been pacing back and forth like a caged tiger, trying to convince himself he'd done the right thing, that if Jamie was too stubborn to listen to reason, he was better off without her.

All he'd asked was that she use a little caution. The trouble was, she was too trusting. She still expected the best from people, despite the fact that those she'd thought were her friends had hurt her badly. Why couldn't she understand that they were like vultures, just waiting to pounce? Maybe she could live that way, never knowing where the next attack was coming from, but he couldn't.

It would be a different matter if the abuse were directed at him. He'd withstood much worse, and he'd developed a thick skin. It wasn't thick enough, though, that he could stand by and watch the woman he loved being hurt. Every barb, every unkind remark or snide, sidelong glance directed her way would be like a dart, piercing his very soul. It was better to break things off cleanly than to put himself through that kind of torture.

Or so he told himself.

Who did he think he was kidding?

With a muttered oath, he grabbed his keys and headed out the door.

She was probably going to think he was crazy, showing up at her door this time of night. Not that he'd blame her. He was surprised at himself. He wasn't in the habit of doing things on the spur of the moment.

This couldn't wait, though. He was seized with a sense of urgency, as if he had to get to Jamie immediately to tell her how much he loved her unconditionally. He wanted her to know he'd marry her in the middle of the intersection of McClintock's main street, with the entire town looking on, if that's what it took to make her happy. And if anyone had any unkind remarks to make, they'd have *him* to deal with. Granted, it wouldn't be easy. The thought of putting himself and Jamie in the limelight that way scared him half to death.

A lifetime without her, though, would be infinitely worse . . .

His attention was diverted by an unusual glow in the sky, over to the west. He frowned slightly as he studied this phenomenon. The sun had gone down hours ago—

He felt a sinking sensation in his stomach as the realization hit him with stunning force. Oblivious to potholes and ruts in the road, he pushed the gas pedal down as far as it would go. The truck shot ahead, the twin shafts of light penetrating the darkness.

Jamie wasn't sure what had awakened her—a sound, a movement, or just a feeling that something was very wrong. Had she simply had a bad dream? Still befuddled from sleep, she pushed herself to a sitting position and tried to separate fantasy from reality.

Alarmed voices reached her, accompanied by a strange, crackling sound. At the same time, she became aware of a flickering light against the bedroom wall. The truth hit her, even before she glanced out the window. Her barn was on fire!

The sight that greeted her as she rushed outside was like something from her worst nightmare. One end of the barn was already engulfed—not the end where the livestock was kept, thank goodness—and flames were starting to lick at the roof. The shrill cries of terrified animals mingled with the crack and sizzle of burning wood.

As she watched, someone ran out of the barn carrying a calf, which he deposited a safe distance away. Several other figures were spraying the structure with water. Their silhouettes were eerie and surreal, and the flames cast distorted shadows on the ground.

At first Jamie was too frozen with shock to do anything except stand and stare in numbed horror. She was galvanized into action by the sight of TJ emerging from the barn, leading a big bay. The horse's nostrils were wide and flaring, and its eyes rolled from side to side. It tossed its head, trying to throw off the firm hand on its halter.

She ran toward TJ, intending to help him, but one of the ranch hands reached him first. Together, the two men managed to calm the skittish creature. "How—what—" Jamie stammered, as the hand led the horse away, talking to him in low, soothing tones.

TJ pulled a handkerchief from his back pocket and wiped his smoke-blackened face. "Val and I spotted it when we were coming back from the dance, and we got over here as quick as we could. Some of the boys were just getting home too, so we got started right away getting the livestock out."

As Jamie eyed the burning structure, she realized there was little point in calling the fire department. By the time help arrived, there wouldn't be much left to salvage. There was no sense in getting them out here in the middle of the night just so they could stand there and watch it burn.

The frantic cries of the animals still in the barn reminded her that there was little time to waste if they hoped to save the rest of the livestock.

TJ glanced over his shoulder in the direction of the plaintive screams. "I'd better get busy." As he turned to go back into the barn, Jamie fell into step beside him. He stopped and looked down at her, rubbing a hand across his chin. A slight frown creased his forehead.

Sensing what was on his mind, Jamie simply said, "They're my animals. My responsibility."

Before TJ could reply, a long, drawn-out whinny, laced with pure terror, pierced the air, a warning to both of them that there was no time to stand around and argue. With a resigned shrug, TJ said, "Let's go, then."

The scene inside the barn was like nothing she could have imagined. Smoke burned her throat and made her eyes water. Faintly, she could make out other figures—looking ghostly and unreal in the haze—struggling to coax frightened animals to safety. She ducked out of the way as a little gelding reared up on its hind legs, emitting a shrill whinny.

She groped her way to the last stall, where a pregnant mare pranced nervously. Panic stabbed through her as she saw, through the smoke, that flames were starting to crawl across the floor of the loft, just above her head. Any minute now, the hay up there would ignite, and when it did, this whole section would come crashing down.

Don't think about it, she told herself. She felt along the wall until her fingers came in contact with the lead rope she knew was hanging on a hook next to the stall. Crooning soothing words—as much for her own reassurance as for the horse's—she clipped the rope to the mare's halter.

But the little mare refused to leave the stall. The harder Jamie tugged on the rope, the more the terrified animal resisted. It was clear Jamie wasn't going to budge her by sheer strength.

Releasing her grip on the rope, she fell to her knees. She knew there was a wooden box somewhere around here. She located it more by touch than by sight, and rummaged around in it until she found a burlap bag. With her fingers trembling so badly they could barely obey her will, she wrapped the bag around the horse's head, so that it covered her eyes, and tied it behind the animal's ears.

Her heart lurched as a crashing noise above her head told her the floor of the loft was getting ready to give way. "Come on," she muttered through clenched teeth, as she pulled harder on the rope. With maddening slowness, the mare took one step, then another.

By now, tears were running down Jamie's cheeks, partly from the smoke and partly from frustration, and her lungs felt as if they would burst if she didn't get a breath of fresh air—

All at once she felt an arm around her waist, like a band of steel, and she was unceremoniously lifted off her feet and tossed to one side. She lost her footing and landed in a heap on the floor.

"Hey, what—" Her angry words were cut off by a tearing, wrenching sound. She watched in horror as a flaming chunk of planking detached itself from the floor of the loft and crashed down. It landed in the spot where she'd been standing just seconds before.

Through the smoke, a tall figure loomed over her and a familiar voice, heavy with concern, asked, "Are you all right?"

"Cole!" She almost sobbed with relief. She accepted the hand he held out to her and scrambled to her feet, resisting the urge to lean against him and absorb some of his strength. There wasn't time for that, even if she had the right. The mare needed her help right now.

As if reading her mind, Cole placed his hands on her shoulders and gave her a gentle but firm push in the direction of the door.

"But the animals—" She was surprised when her words came out in a hoarse, ragged whisper. She took a deep breath so she could try again, but she only drew smoke into her lungs. Everything around her started to swirl, and she felt herself swaying.

Cole thrust her into the arms of someone nearby—she had no idea who. "Get her out of here," he barked.

Meekly, she let herself be led away. She had no strength left to protest.

Although she had no recollection of leaving the barn, she found herself sitting on the back step. Her head began to clear as she inhaled deep drafts of fresh air. She was vaguely aware that Val was sitting next to her, watching her closely. She wanted to say, *Don't worry, I'm not going to pass out,* but breathing seemed to be all she could manage at the moment.

As rational thought started to return, it brought with it a sense of urgency. She should be doing her part instead of just sitting here.

Val's arm came around her shoulders, comforting as well as gently restraining. "They're doing all they can," she said in a soothing voice.

Val was right, of course. By now all the animals had been brought out, and the other outbuildings were being hosed down so the fire wouldn't spread to them. There was nothing left for her to do—except sit here and watch her barn burn to the ground.

Replacing it, along with the hay in the loft, was going to put a major dent in her budget, but it couldn't be helped. She could get by without a barn for now, but she'd have to have one once winter came on. And she still had one more cutting of hay before the season was over. She had to have someplace to store it.

She gave a philosophical shrug. It wouldn't do any good to bemoan the fact that, like many of the other ranchers in the area, her parents had opted to drop the insurance on the aged structure the last time the rates had gone up. She could have reinstated it herself, of course, but there had been so many other expenses.

"Keep back. It's gonna go any minute!" The sudden shout caused her to look up. The building was now fully engulfed. Before her eyes it became a mere skeleton of charred, blackened timbers, as the flames ate away at the walls, the roof.

She watched in mute horror as those timbers swayed, then crashed to the ground, sending up a shower of sparks and ashes.

Chapter Sixteen

Jamie noticed with surprise that faint streaks of pink were breaking through the darkness. The storm that had threatened last night had failed to materialize.

TJ and Val and the others had left, to go to their respective beds or bunks for some much-needed rest. They'd all gone above and beyond the call of duty, and she'd be eternally grateful for all their help, but they'd done everything that could be done for now. There was no reason for them to stay any longer.

Still, as she stood in the deserted barnyard dispiritedly regarding the smoldering remains of what had been her barn, she'd never felt more alone in her life.

"There, that should last them for a while."

Jamie gave a start at the sound of Cole's voice. She glanced over her shoulder, to see him coming up behind her. It occurred to her that he was a beautiful sight, even as disheveled as he was, smelling of smoke and ashes, with his hair slightly singed and his eyes still red-rimmed.

"I—I thought you'd gone with the others."

"No, I was just making sure the animals had enough food and water."

She reminded herself that he'd only stayed behind when the others had left out of a sense of neighborly obligation. Still, his calm, matter-of-fact strength was just what she needed right now.

She felt incredibly tired. It was a weariness of the mind and spirit as well as the body. Before long she would have to tackle the monumental task of figuring out how she was going to replace her barn. For the time being, though, she felt incapable of making even the simplest decision.

She drew in her breath in a long, ragged sigh.

Cole glanced down at her. That sigh, along with the disheartened slump of her shoulders, made him ache to take her in his arms and comfort her. He wasn't sure what her reaction would be, though, after the harsh words he'd said to her last night—just before he'd walked out. A stab of pain shot through him at the memory.

He put one arm around her, tentatively, and drew her toward him, half expecting her to stiffen up and pull away. Relief flooded through him as she came to him with no resistance. And when she rested her cheek against his chest in that trusting way . . .

It felt so good to hold her. It took all the restraint he had to limit himself to patting her gently and murmuring soothing words. He didn't want to take advantage of her vulnerability. Later, after she'd had time to recover from the shock of seeing her barn burn to the ground, they'd talk of . . . other things.

Jamie felt strength flowing into her weary mind and body as she stood in the circle of Cole's embrace. This was where she belonged . . .

But he was simply offering a bit of comfort, she reminded herself. It didn't mean a thing. Hadn't he made his feelings quite clear—had it just been last night? It seemed a lifetime ago.

Summoning her last remaining reserves of will power, she twisted out of his arms. "Come up to the house," she said briskly. "I'll fix you some breakfast."

Over bacon and eggs, Cole asked, "Do you have any idea what caused the fire?"

"I—I suppose it was from the heat lightning. With all that hay in the barn, it wouldn't have taken much."

"You sound kind of doubtful. Is there any other way you think it might have started?"

Jamie wrapped her hands around her coffee cup to steady them. She would rather not mention Randy's late-night visit. What good would it do? What was done was done. Cole was looking at her expectantly, though.

"After you . . . left last night I went out to the barn. While I was there, Randy showed up."

"Randy was here?" Jamie noticed that his tone suddenly changed, and that the muscles tightened along his jawline. "What did he want?"

Jamie shrugged. "He was just being his usual trouble-making self. I made it quite clear to him that I wanted no part of him. He didn't seem inclined to leave, so I just walked off and left him standing there in the barn."

"And?" Cole prompted.

"He was smoking. I made him put his cigarette out, but he was starting to light another one when I left."

"Then you think he could have started the fire?"

Jamie looked down at her hands. "With everything else that's happened, I really haven't gotten around to giving it any thought until now. It does seem likely, though. Oh, I don't think he'd do it on purpose—that would be a new low, even for Randy. But—well, common sense was never his strong point.'' She could picture him carelessly tossing his cigarette aside, without bothering to make sure it was out.

Cole took a long drink of his coffee. Finally, he asked, ''What do you plan to do about this?''

''I don't know,'' she admitted. ''All I have are my suspicions. If I make any accusations against Randy, it won't be long before the whole town knows he was here last night. I . . .''

She'd started to say she simply wasn't up to facing any more gossip, but this was an area she'd rather not get into with Cole if she could help it. She was sure he was well aware, just as she was, that the subject of gossip, and the town's propensity for it, was what had come between them.

''Anyway,'' she finished up lamely, ''it could have been the lightning.''

She got up and went to the stove to get the coffeepot. She hoped he didn't notice how her hands were trembling as she refilled his cup.

When she sat back down she said, ''I want you to know how much I appreciate all your help last night.''

He lifted one shoulder in a dismissive shrug, as if to say, It was nothing.

''I couldn't help wondering, though,'' she went on, ''how did you know about the fire?''

''I saw the glow in the sky.''

Jamie gave him a puzzled look. ''From your place?'' There was a ridge of hills that separated the two ranches.

''No, I . . . ah . . . I was already on my way back here.''

What exactly did he mean by that? She waited for him to offer some kind of explanation.

Seconds ticked away as the silence lengthened. She got up and went over to the counter, where she made a few ineffectual swipes with the dishcloth. "Wh—why were you coming back?" she finally asked, her back to him. "Did you forget something?"

"I guess you could say that."

Jamie heard his chair scrape along the floor as if he were pushing it away from the table. She could sense his presence as he came up to stand behind her, she could feel his warm breath on her hair. She hardly dared move when he put his hands on her shoulders.

"What I 'forgot' is that my life isn't worth two cents without you," he whispered. "I must have been crazy to walk out on you that way. If we love each other enough, this is something we can work out." His lips were very close to her ear. She couldn't suppress the little shiver that ran through her.

Very gently, he turned her around so she was facing him. She couldn't have offered any resistance even if she'd wanted to. Her bones felt as if they were melting like warm candle wax.

"I was coming back to tell you it doesn't matter to me where we get married, or if we have the entire state of Oregon at our wedding." His voice was low and earnest. "I just want to be married to you."

She wanted to reassure him that she'd marry him under any terms he wanted, but she couldn't speak for the lump in her throat. She could only look at him helplessly. He seemed to understand what was in her heart, though. She wasn't sure which of them made the first move, but somehow she was in his arms. She felt as if she'd come home.

"I was afraid I'd lost you," he whispered, in a tone husky with emotion, "because of my stubbornness."

"Oh Cole, It was all my fault—"

"Shh." He put a finger to her lips. "You'll have to be patient with me, you know. I've been a loner for so long that I'm not sure I know how to be any other way. Sometimes I get as prickly as a porcupine when I feel things are closing in on me. I'll do my best, but it may take me a while to learn to be a—a social butterfly." His mouth twisted into a lopsided grin that caused her heart to do flip-flops.

He pulled away just enough that he could look down into her eyes. "I want to do it right this time."

"What—what do you mean?"

Releasing her, he placed one hand over his heart. "Jamie Cantrell," he intoned solemnly, "will you do me the honor of marrying me in the McClintock Community Church, with the entire population of McClintock in attendance?"

"I'll marry you wherever you say. And I'll live with you in a cave, or a desert island, or—or—"

Her words were cut off by the sound of tires on gravel.

Looking over Cole's shoulder, Jamie glanced out the window. "It's probably Val and TJ coming back to see if I need any—" Her eyes widened in surprise.

Cole lifted an eyebrow quizzically, then turned to see what had captured her attention. As his gaze followed hers, he muttered an exclamation under his breath. "We'd better go see what this is all about," he said, taking Jamie's hand.

When they stepped out the back door they looked at one another in amazement. A procession of flatbeds, pickups and other vehicles was coming down the long driveway. As the caravan made its way to the backyard, Jamie could see that most of them were carrying an assortment of lumber and other building supplies. One large truck held a load of hay, and the end of the procession was brought up by a bulldozer.

As Jamie stared, speechless, Joe Keeler hopped down from the lead truck and ambled over to where she stood with Cole. "We . . . uh . . . heard about your misfortune," he said, briefly touching the brim of his hat in greeting. "We came to build you a barn."

"How . . . how did you . . ." Jamie stammered.

"Word gets around." This was from Ed Sutter, who had come up behind Joe. "Me'n my boys can put up a barn faster'n you can say Jack Sprat." He looked over his shoulder at his two strapping sons, who were already unloading their tools from the back of his pickup.

As other vehicles pulled into the yard, Joe, who apparently had been appointed spokesperson, said, "In the old days, when this area was being settled, folks could put up a barn in one day, when they all worked together to help each other. I don't see no reason why we still can't do it." He spoke quickly, as if anxious to get the talking over with and get to the business at hand. Like most of the men around here, he preferred "doing" to "talking about it."

"We got to get it done in a day," Ed put in. "Del Ramsey brought a load of hay—to replace what was in your loft, ma'am. We have to have a place to store it."

"We can get started as soon as Len clears away the rubble," Joe said briskly, glancing toward Len Hubley, who sat aboard his bulldozer.

It took a little while for Jamie to grasp that all these men and women—her neighbors and lifelong friends—were here for an old-fashioned barn raising.

She glanced at the faces of those gathered in her backyard—not just fellow ranchers, but townsfolk as well. She recognized some of the people who had stood by and watched last night, without uttering a word in her defense, when Aunt Nadine was saying all those terrible things to her. She spotted Ida Simms, who had been on the school board when she'd been asked to resign. Of course, she'd never known if any of the board members had believed in her innocence, but if any of them had, they obviously hadn't argued very convincingly on her behalf. And—wonder of wonders—there was Roy Mayfield, looking somewhat shamefaced.

There were others she wouldn't have expected to come to her aid, people who, although they hadn't exactly shunned her, hadn't rushed to support her either.

Sudden tears sprung to her eyes. "Thank you all, so much . . ." was all she could get out. She knew if she tried to say anything more her voice would break.

"No need to thank us," Joe said. "Neighbors have to stick together." He cleared his throat self-consciously, then turned around and called out, "Let's start getting this stuff unloaded. We've got a lot of work to do."

In a matter of minutes the yard was alive with activity. As everyone went about their assigned duties, one woman stepped up to Jamie and patted her arm. "Sometimes it's hard for folks around here to say they're sorry, honey. Just keep in mind, actions speak louder than words." With that, she turned and hurried off before Jamie could reply.

As Jamie watched her leave, she thought over the simple statement. It was unlikely that any of these people were going to come to her and offer an apology for the way they'd treated her, or admit they were wrong in believing those stories about her. What they *were* saying, though, by rallying around her in her time of need, was that it didn't matter. She was one of their own.

Oh, she didn't doubt there would always be some who would steadfastly refuse to believe in her innocence. But those who were important to her knew she wasn't guilty of any wrongdoing. And the others? Somehow, it no longer mattered as much as it once did.

"Hey, Wyatt," Ed Sutter called out as he walked by carrying a toolbox, "you any good at carpentry?"

Jamie wondered how Cole was taking all this. Hesitantly,

she stole a glance at him. It was impossible to tell from his expression what was on his mind.

Considering his long-standing commitment to being self-sufficient, to taking care of things by himself without accepting help from others, would he resent what he might think of as "interference?" He might feel this was something between the two of them, that they handle themselves. True, he'd promised her, just a little while ago, to do his best to overcome his "lone wolf" tendencies. That sounded good in theory, but she doubted if he'd expected to be called on to put it into practice so soon. He'd likely hoped to "ease into" his new role gradually.

She held her breath, waiting for his response to Ed's question.

Her apprehension turned to relief as Cole called back, "As a matter of fact, I swing a pretty mean hammer. Be with you in a minute."

He turned to Jamie. "But first . . ." he whispered. In full view of the entire group, he took her in his arms. "I think we were about to seal our engagement with a kiss, before we were interrupted."

As his lips met hers, the people in her backyard, the trucks and other vehicles, all faded away. Jamie loved him so much at this moment she felt some kind of soft, gentle glow must be radiating from her, visible for everybody to see.

They were reluctantly brought back from the private little world into which they'd retreated by the sound of cheering, and a long, low, wolf whistle. "Okay, break it up," someone called out. "It's time to get to work."

"We'll finish this later," Cole murmured huskily. His eyes held an unspoken promise that sent a little shiver of anticipation through her.

Cole jumped nimbly down from the porch to join the group of neighbors and friends assembled in the yard. As they moved aside to make room for him, Jamie's heart was so full of joy she was sure it would overflow.